IN JACK'S
ARMS

Fighting Connollys, Book 2

Roxie Rivera

Night Works Books
College Station, Texas

Night Works Books
3515-B Longmire Drive #103
College Station, Texas 77845
www.roxierivera.com

Publisher's Note: This is a work of fiction. Names, characters, places, and incidents are a product of the author's imagination. Locales and public names are sometimes used for atmospheric purposes. Any resemblance to actual people, living or dead, or to businesses, companies, events, institutions, or locales is completely coincidental.

Book Layout ©2013 BookDesignTemplates.com

Ordering Information:
Quantity sales. Special discounts are available on quantity purchases by corporations, associations, and others. For details, contact the "Special Sales Department" at the address above.

In Jack's Arms (Fighting Connollys #2)/ Roxie Rivera. -- 1st ed.
ISBN 978-1-63042-019-2

For David, light of my life, fire of my loins,
bringer of soda and child wrangler
extraordinaire

1 Chapter one

Exhausted and suffering from an aching back, I rubbed my blurry eyes and tried to focus on the serial number etched into the bottom of the DVD player so I could compare it to the pawn ticket tag. Conducting a spur of the moment inventory on thousands of items in our storeroom? It wasn't exactly the way I wanted to spend my Monday, but an overnight break-in and burglary had pretty much scuttled my plans.

"Hey, Abby?" Mark, one of my brokers, poked his head into the backroom. "One of our regulars is here. He's trying to pawn a silver chain but..."

"It's under weight?"

"Yeah. I wouldn't bother you with it, but he's one of our best customers. I know you like to give them a break every now and then."

"Who is it?"

"Big Carl."

"Oh." I thought of the sweet older man who took care of his ailing mama. She was torn up with diabetes and on dialysis, and he was barely scraping by with his hardware store job. "What's he want?"

"He wants eighty, but I was thinking of giving him, like, thirty-five or forty."

"It's the end of the month, Mark. I bet he's trying to scrape together enough money for his mama's meds. Give him the eighty. He's good for it."

I didn't say what we were both thinking. On the first, Carl would start receiving the disability and Social Security deposits that kept their household just this side of the poverty line. Like many pawn shops, Kirkwood's Jewelry and Loan provided a needed service to folks who required a little extra money to tie together the ends of their dwindling budgets.

There weren't a lot of choices for households on the fringe. They could come through my front door, pawn a television or watch, and walk out with some cash to be repaid at a high but fair interest rate, or they could take their chances with one of the payday loan places that were popping up all over the place. The really desperate ones visited loan sharks like Besian Beciraj or John Hagen, although the latter was rumored to be winding up the illicit side of his business.

Mark looked less than thrilled with my decision but shrugged. "Whatever you say, boss lady."

He didn't say it meanly, but I sensed he didn't approve of the small favors I did for our regular customers every now and then. He had been at the shop only a few years and had come from a personal finance place across town that did things differently. I had learned the business by trailing my granddad around the store as a kid. Customer loyalty and word of mouth were huge in this trade, and I leapt at any chance to ensure both.

Letting it go, I got back to work comparing the serial numbers and pawn tags in our company database to the items remaining on our shelves. Since being called up to the shop just after six that morning, I had crawled and climbed and sifted through hundreds of items. I had never been more thankful for Granddad insisting on upgrading to barcodes and scanners a few years ago. This ordeal had been bad enough that the thought of having to manually flip through the inventory logs made me want to weep!

A knock at the storeroom door interrupted my work. The police and insurance crew had been in and out of the shop all day, but it was nearly seven in the evening so I doubted it was either of those two paying me a visit at this hour. Wiping my dusty hands on the towel slung over my shoulder, I crossed to the door and wrenched it open. The jovial, handsome face of Detective Eric Santos greeted me. "Hey!"

"Hi, Abby." He gestured to the storeroom behind me. "Would it be all right if I came in to chat for a few minutes?"

"Sure." I stepped aside and motioned for him to join me. "It's been a while since you've visited the shop. Not since those punks in the 1-8-7 crew tried to unload all those stolen cell phones, right?"

"Has it been that long?" He shook his head and raised his eyebrows. "Man, that's been seven months? Eight?"

"About that," I said. "Granddad was still puttering around the place."

The corners of his mouth dipped with sadness. "I still have a hard time believing Mr. K is gone. I walked in the door and expected to see him behind the counter, to hear him laughing and telling his stories."

"It's been five months, and I still do the same thing, Eric." Feeling a fresh wave of grief welling up inside him, I quickly changed the subject. "So, are you working the robbery beat now?"

He leaned back against one of the sturdy shelves. "No, I'm still working guns and gangs."

"But this was a robbery. Unless..." I put two-and-two together and exhaled roughly. "You think this break-in last night was gang related?"

"I do."

"Eric, they didn't take anything useful. They totally bypassed the big-ticket items like jewelry and electronics. They didn't even try to get to the firearms. All they took were the video cameras and cell phones."

He frowned. "That's all?"

I nodded. "So far that's the only thing that's missing back here. What kind of a gang robs a store full of expensive, easy to fence jewelry and doesn't even take a single gold chain?"

"You've seen some of the dumbasses who run with the crews around here." Eric shot me a troubling look. "Of course, this might have been a message."

"From?"

"You're in a tricky spot here, Abby. You've got the Hermanos that way and the 1-8-7 crew that way." He gestured to his left and right with his thumb. "Now that John Hagen is getting out of the sharking game, the word is that the Albanians are pushing down into this territory."

Nothing that Eric said was a revelation to me. I had lived and worked in this neighborhood long enough to know all the angles and all the power players. "I doubt it's the Albanians."

"Yeah, because they're such warm and fuzzy guys."

"I don't know about warm and fuzzy, but I've never had problems with any of them."

"Probably because your granddad used to play nice with Afrim Barisha before he got himself shot and stuffed in a trunk," Eric brusquely replied. "Don't think I don't know about all that under the table dealing those two did."

"I wouldn't know a thing about that." I did, actually, know quite a bit about the way Granddad used to take payments for the Albanian loan shark who operated out of the backroom of a bar a few blocks over from us. After inheriting the business, I put a stop to it, but I had managed to maintain a cordial relationship with Besian Beciraj, the mob captain who had stepped in to fill the power void.

"You had better not," Eric gently warned. "That's not a world you want to get mixed up in, Abby. It's dark and dangerous business. Stick to pawning and making loans. It's safer."

I considered some of the violent and threatening customers who came through the front door. "Some days."

"Fair enough." He conceded that fact with a smile. "Look, I'm going to keep an eye on this case. To me, this burglary was part of a bigger pattern. You had an attempted break-in a few weeks ago and then this real break-in last night. They stole from you but not enough to hurt you. Someone is trying to intimidate you—and who is more likely than Besian?"

"He doesn't need to intimidate me. Our business models are totally different. I operate on the right side of the law, and he operates on the wrong one."

"It could be about a protection tax."

"Well, I'm a skilled negotiator, Eric. I've got this one."

"Don't be so cocky, Abby. You can't do everything on your own."

"I've done a pretty good job so far." Eric knew only too well what sort of childhood I had survived before Granddad had stepped in to adopt me and my older brother. At a very early age, I had learned that I could count on no one but myself, and that I needed to be able to talk my way out of any situation. "We'll be fine, but I really appreciate you showing so much concern."

"This pawn shop has been around since the fifties, and your family is one of the oldest in this neighborhood. The businesses on this block are the main reason this area has stayed safe and prosperous. I want it to stay that way."

"So do I."

Eric signaled the end of that discussion with a short bob of his head. "So how is Mattie doing? I'll

admit I was upset that he wasn't placed on my baseball team this year. I really miss him at short stop,
and no one trash talks from the dugout like Mattie."

I grinned at the funny memories Eric evoked. For
the last four years, the detective had been coaching a
special needs baseball team every summer. The program had gotten so popular that they had added two
more coaches and teams this year. "Mattie was sad
that he didn't make your team, but he seems to really
enjoy Jack and Finn's coaching style."

Eric issued a throaty sound of annoyance and rolled
his eyes. "Yeah, yeah. Everyone loves those Connolly
brothers." He gave a snort of amusement. "At the rate
the bleachers are filling with single ladies, these games
are going to be standing room only soon. If the women
hanging around the parking lot after the games are
any indication, Jack might be the hottest bachelor in
Houston this summer."

I ignored the sharp bite of jealousy that Eric's
words inspired. The mere mention of Jack Connolly
sent a wicked swooping sensation through my belly.
Like his two younger brothers, Finn and Kelly, Jack
was something of a legend around this neighborhood.
He had been an officer in the Marine Corps and had
completed two tours in Afghanistan and two in Iraq.
But that was before his convoy rolled over an IED,

and he sustained a head injury that forced him out of the job he had loved so much.

Four years ago, he had returned to Houston to take over the family gym. Granddad had given him a series of small loans over that first year to help Jack make payroll and improvements. Since that first morning he had walked into the shop to pawn that motorcycle he had loved so much, I hadn't been able to shake my immediate and incredibly strong attraction to the dark-haired, green-eyed fighter. I had absolutely no business at all fantasizing about the smolderingly sexy former Marine who taught my weekly self-defense class, but I couldn't help myself.

Hiding my interest in Jack, I said simply, "He's a nice guy. They both are."

"They are," he agreed. "I think it's important for our players to see someone like Finn living a full, happy life. He doesn't let his missing leg stop him from going after life full force, you know?"

"Absolutely." I couldn't help but smile as I remembered the Saturday morning practice session when Mattie had gotten his first look at Finn's prosthesis. "I almost died from embarrassment when Mattie asked Finn if he was a cyborg."

Eric laughed. "That sounds like Mattie, all right. What did Finn say?"

"He told Mattie to keep his secret because the government didn't want everyone to know about their super soldiers."

"I bet Mattie just ate that right up."

"He loved it. I don't think I've seen him laugh that hard in a long time." Ever since our granddad had finally succumbed to his congestive heart failure, Mattie had been withdrawn and temperamental. All that changed when the baseball team had started practicing in early May. "He's happier lately and spending a lot of time at Connolly Fitness."

"I doubt Jack or Finn mind that at all."

"At first, I was worried he would overstay his welcome, but Jack assured me they all enjoy Mattie's company."

"That's good. I know Mattie is in that odd phase where he's too old for school—and he loved high school—and too young and independent for the residential programs around town."

My younger brother's Down Syndrome diagnosis had hampered his earliest years, when our mother was more concerned about finding her next fix than getting him to occupational or physical therapy. After moving in with Granddad, Mattie had finally gotten the help he had needed to thrive. "I'm thrilled he's making new friends and feeling out the real world in his own way. I don't worry nearly as much because I trust that Jack and Finn will keep an eye on him."

"Hell, with two Marines as his bodyguards, he's the safest kid in town."

"Let's hope."

Eric's phone began to ring, and he fished it out of his pocket. When he glanced at the screen, he frowned but didn't answer before shoving it away. "I've got to run. I'll follow up with you in a day or two. When are you submitting your final report to the station?"

"Wednesday morning," I said, trailing him to the door. "I should have the inventory completed by to-morrow night." Even though I was certain he was overreaching on his gang tie suspicion, I asked, "Would you like a copy?"

He shook his head. "I'll grab one from the detectives on this case. I'd like to come by and look at the security footage."

"There isn't any."

Eric looked taken aback. "How is that possible?"

"Dan forgot to switch on the security system when he closed down the store on Sunday evening. That's how these thieves were able to get in and out unno-ticed."

"I hope you're going to dock his pay for that."

"It was an honest mistake."

Eric didn't look convinced. "I'll follow up with you if I hear anything troubling on the street."

"I would appreciate that." I opened the door and leaned against it. "Thanks for checking on us, Eric."

"Happy to serve," he said with a grin. Two steps into the office area of the shop, he paused and turned back to me. "There was a warrant roundup this morning. You know what that means."

"Ugh." My shoulders dropped as I imagined the crowd that would be waiting at my door in the morning. "It means I'm going to have a line of mamas and girlfriends trying to pawn everything they own in the morning to raise bail money."

He smirked teasingly. "Hey, that's your bread and butter, right?"

"Get out of here," I said and shooed him. "Or else I'll call the cops on you for criminal mischief."

Chuckling, Eric waved at me and disappeared into the main area of the shop. I popped into our finance manager's office and waited for her to finish up the note she was making before asking her to request extra cash from the bank before she clocked out. In the final days of the month, we always experienced an upswing in loan demand, and with the added surge of customers who typically came to us when they needed to bond out their relatives, I hated the idea of running low on cash when we needed it most.

After a quick chat with the employees on the night shift, I returned to the storeroom and picked up where I'd left off on the inventory. Just as I was getting really sick of numbers and barcodes, Dan, the night manager, called out to me. "Abby, you in here somewhere?"

"At the back, in stereos and speakers," I shouted. "What do you need?"

"Where is Mattie?"

"His shift ended at four. He's probably at the gym. Why?"

Shuffling feet on concrete heralded Dan's arrival at the line of shelves behind me. "Was Mattie pulling past due tickets today?"

"Yes. I asked him to go through and pull everything that was a week beyond the grace period. Those customers have had ample time to come in and renew the loan or pay off the balance."

I scanned a barcode and steeled myself for the inevitable disagreement I knew was coming. Dan had been with the shop for nearly as long as I had been alive, but he didn't agree with my decision to allow Mattie to work with us. If Dan had his way, Mattie would only be allowed to clean the glass cases or sweep the place. My brother could do so much more—and I intended to make sure he got the chance to prove himself.

"Well, he seems to have taken some of the merchandise from the shop."

"What?" I stepped into the small walking space between shelves so I could see Dan. "What did he take?"

"A watch."

"Whose watch was it?"

"Nick Connolly's."

"Oh." The elder Connolly had been a longtime customer of the shop, and a few months earlier, he had come in to pawn a watch to raise some quick cash. To pay his light bill, he had said, but I had suspected it was for a card game. Between his alcoholism and gambling addiction, the old guy was a damned mess, but I hoped the bullet he had recently taken while trying to save his youngest son's girlfriend might put him on the wagon for good. "I'm sure he thought he was helping friends."

"He can't do that, Abby. It's property of the shop, and that's on our books. We can't keep the doors open if your brother is skipping off with inventory whenever he pleases. This is why I don't like him messing with my stuff. He isn't smart enough to—"

"Dan," I interrupted him as respectfully as possible even though I was steaming inside. "First, it's not *your* stuff. It's the store's stuff. Second, I'm quite aware of how the pawn business works and how to balance our books and inventory. My business degree sort of covered all that. As for Mattie taking the watch, I'm sure this was an isolated case. He's never taken a thing from this store, not even a pencil from my desk, without asking permission two or three times. That's just the way he is."

"Well—I don't like it."

I bit my tongue rather than reminding him where he could go if he didn't. "Mattie is a Kirkwood, and this is our family's business. He belongs here. End of story. Okay?"

Dan sighed. "Sure. Fine."

"I'll sort out the watch situation."

"I'm sure you will," he grumbled on his way back to the front of the shop.

Setting aside the barcode scanner and logbook, I found a stack of crates to sit on and rubbed my temples for a few seconds. Exhaling with frustration, I tugged my cell phone from the pocket of my jeans and dialed Mattie's number. Five rings later, someone finally answered, but it wasn't my brother.

"Hi, Abby."

I blinked as the gruff, rumbling waves of Jack Connolly's voice rolled through me. A girlish quiver of giddiness filtered through my belly and into my chest. "Hey, Jack. Um...I guess that answers my question about Mattie's whereabouts."

"He's here. I've got him doing circuits. Do you need him?"

"No, it can wait." I suddenly found myself wishing I had some other reason to keep Jack on the line. Man, how pathetic! I was pining over a man who only saw me as a client of his gym and the big sister of one of his players. Jack was so outrageously sexy that women were literally falling at his feet. A girl like me? I had no chance with a man like that.

I had seen the women he chatted up after class and around the baseball fields. They were blue or green-eyed beauties with killer curves and mega sex appeal. Me? I was basically the exact opposite of those girls with my cocoa skin, dark eyes and jet black curly hair. Instead of a knockout figure, I had a petite body with breasts that barely filled a B cup and a tiny booty that no amount of squats had yet to make big or deli-cious despite all the promises of those fitness DVDs.

"Abby?"

"Yes?"

"Are you okay? Mattie told me about the robbery." He hesitated. "If you need anything—"

"They only took some video cameras. It was noth-ing big. We've already had the doors and locks re-placed, and our security system has been revamped. We'll bounce back."

"I wasn't talking about the store, Abby. I was talking about *you*. Are you okay?"

The concern deepening his voice knocked me for a loop. "Yes, I'm fine."

"You know it's okay to *not* be fine sometimes, Abby. It doesn't make you weak to ask for some support from close friends."

"Like you?" The words rushed out of my mouth before I could even reconsider them. Were we close friends? I hoped so but...

"Of course like me, Abby." He paused for a few seconds. "You and Mattie are very important to me."

"We are?" God, I hated how stupid I sounded. *Get a grip, Abs!*

"Yes, you are. If you didn't know that, I'm obviously doing something wrong."

I swallowed hard and tried not to read into his comment. With my stress-fried brain, it would be only too easy to misinterpret this and make a real jackass of myself.

"Listen, when Mattie is finished working out, I'll bring him back to the shop. I'll swing by and grab some takeout, okay? Let me treat you guys to dinner. It's been a long day."

"Oh, Jack, you don't have to—"

"I want to, Abby," he cut in gently. "I'll send you a text when we leave. All right?"

"Um...sure."

"Great. See you later."

"Bye."

Staring at my phone, I tried to make sense of what had just happened. *We're important to him?* My fatigued brain dredged up all the run-ins I'd had with Jack over the last four years as he dragged his family's gym out of near bankruptcy to make it a raging success. After Granddad's health had started to go downhill, I seemed to see more of Jack. Now that I thought about it, I wondered if that was by design—*his* design.

All those late nights he had turned up at the shop to browse the firearms and go through our sports inventory suddenly seemed less than coincidental. How many times had he just happened to swing by when I was working late by myself or with only one other employee? How many times had he picked up a broom or mop to help me finish with closing?

I glanced up at the fluorescent light bulbs overhead and remembered the way he had taken it upon himself to install them after running into me at the hardware store a few weeks ago. Never in my wildest dreams would I have dared to think that simple act of kindness was something else.

Was it really possible that devastatingly handsome Jack wanted *me*?

2 CHAPTER TWO

Swinging side to side in his office chair, Jack Connolly stared at Mattie's phone. Abby's sweet voice ricocheted round and round in his head. How the hell had he screwed up things so badly that Abby didn't even realize how much her safety meant to him?

Still clutching Mattie's phone, he shoved out of his chair and crossed his office to the window that gave him an unimpeded view of the gym. He braced his palm against the cool glass and watched the two dozen or so clients moving through the various stations. Unlike some of the gyms that catered to high-end clientele with their sleek machines and expensive trainers,

Connolly Fitness embraced an old-school feel with its minimalist design and wide open space.

Most clients followed a challenging conditioning and strengthening regimen that consisted of cardio, weight lifting, and flexibility work. He made use of his contacts from his military days to hire instructors to teach self-defense and fighting classes like Krav Maga, kickboxing, Muay Thai, and Eskrima. They had a mixed-martial arts program that was just over a year old and more popular than ever. Finally, after years of busting his ass, the gym was operating fully in the black.

But a few weeks earlier, they had come uncomfortably close to losing it all. Their father had gotten them tangled up in a mess of debts to two different loan sharks, one of them with a claim on the building itself. Jack's chest tightened when he thought of the way his younger brother's girlfriend had saved their backsides by giving the loan shark the building she had planned to use as the headquarters for her growing tech business.

The tightness in his chest increased when he remembered the night he and Kelly had barely managed to save her from that psycho stalker while their dad bled out on the floor of her apartment after taking a bullet to protect her. Their old man had held on through a night of surgeries and was now in recovery at home. Though he respected his father for risking his life for Bee's, Jack still had incredibly complicated feelings toward him. The years of abuse their family had suffered under that alcoholic bastard's hands were too much for him to forgive and forget.

Mattie's deep belly laugh drew Jack from his thoughts. The laughter punctuated the heavy metal Finn liked to play over the sound system in the evenings. Abby's baby brother hugged his stomach as he guffawed at something funny he had heard from the three guys he had been doing burpees beside. No doubt the joke or story he had just been told was dirty and wholly inappropriate. He had asked the guys who worked out with Mattie to watch their language, but his request didn't seem to stick for very long.

Though he wanted to shield Mattie from the coarser side of male camaraderie, he was glad that the gym's clients all respected and accepted the younger man. Jack had made it perfectly clear that he would kick the ass of any person who spoke badly of or rudely toward Mattie. Kelly and Finn would take turns whooping some ass when he was finished. So far, he hadn't had to follow through on that threat. Mattie's friendliness and sense of humor were so damned endearing even the roughest ex-Special Forces guys who trained at the gym couldn't help but smile when he was near.

Jack stepped into the gym. "Mattie! Do your cool down and hit the showers, man."

Mattie waved to let him know that he'd received his order and started the final phase of his workout. Jack slipped back inside his office and tidied up his desk. As they inevitably did, his thoughts circled back to Abby. Like him, she was a workaholic, but he had his two brothers to keep him in line. Who did Abby have to watch her back and keep her from burning out with exhaustion?

From the moment Mr. Kirkwood had gotten sick and started the long, slow slide toward hospice, Jack had been constantly worried about Abby. His stomach just churned when he thought of the burdens she silently bore. Supporting her granddad as he started the final journey of his life, stepping into the old man's shoes to run the pawn shop, taking over as Mattie's guardian—it was a whole hell of a lot of stress for one woman to endure.

Not for the first time, he questioned his decision to give her some space and approach her slowly. He would be a damned liar if he said he hadn't been head over heels for Abby since the moment he spied her in the pawn shop that morning he had come in to beg for a short-term loan from her grandfather. That megawatt smile of hers had nearly knocked him on his ass.

Falling for a college student had been the very last thing he had ever expected that morning.

Her age and his respect for her grandfather had been the two main reasons he hadn't pursued his interest in her at the time. Newly discharged from the Corps he had loved so much, he hadn't been in the best place emotionally or mentally back then. She had deserved better than a short-tempered, rough bastard who couldn't sleep through the night.

But watching her date other men hadn't been easy. Every time he worked up the courage to finally make a move, the timing was wrong. When she had been free for the asking, he had been committed to saving their family's legacy, building a loyal clientele, and helping Finn get off the booze and into a treatment program. She had been dating some hotshot law school guy when he finally had some room in his schedule and his life to do right by wooing her. Just when he thought the universe had aligned, her granddad got sick and passed away, and then his own father was mired in some messy shit with the Albanians and John Hagen.

What if there wasn't a perfect time? What if he had fucked it all up by not going after the woman he wanted? Jack swiped his keys and wallet from his drawer and gruffly swore, "Shit!"

"We're not supposed to use that word, Jack." Freshly showered and holding his gym bag, Mattie stood in the doorway of the office with a censorious expression. "You owe a dollar to the swear jar."

"A dollar!" Jack reacted with mock outrage. "Jesus, when I was a kid, it was a quarter."

"Well, you're old and that's the cost of inflation."

"I'm not *that* old, Mattie."

"You're thirty."

"Thirty-three," he corrected. "And that's still not old."

"It's older than me."

"Fair enough." Jack reached for his own gym bag and handed over Mattie's phone. "Your sister called earlier. Did you forget to tell her that you were coming here?"

"Uh-oh." Mattie made a face. "Was she mad?"

"No. She sounded concerned."

"You're sure she wasn't mad?"

"Why would she be mad at you?"

"I broke a rule."

"What rule?"

"A shop rule." Mattie hesitated and then unzipped a side pouch on his bag. He produced a watch that was only too familiar to Jack. "I took this from the shop."

Jack fought the urge to snatch the watch his mother had worked so hard to buy for their father all those Christmases ago. Instead he held out his hand and let Mattie gently place it on his palm. He turned it over and ran his finger across the inscription there. The memories of his gentle, sweet mother created a throbbing ball of pain that choked off his throat. The guilt of missing her funeral while he was away at war still ate at him.

"Did Pop pawn this?"

Mattie nodded. "He forgot to pay."

"So you took it?"

"Nick is my friend. He always brings me those sour candies I like."

Jack made a mental note to remind his father to stop doing that. Mattie went through life thinking the very best of everyone when reality was so much meaner. He hated the idea of Nick conditioning Mattie to accept gifts in exchange for favors. It could lead to some dangerous places.

"Abby put four extensions on the loan," Mattie continued, "but it was in the pull stack for this week."

"The pull stack?"

"It's what we call the stuff we take out of the back and put up for sale in the store."

Irritation raced through him as he realized how close their family had come to losing this watch because of their father's reckless selfishness. "We'll swing by the shop, and I'll make this right."

Seeing the uncertainty on Mattie's face, he reached out and squeezed the younger's man's shoulder. "I appreciate what you did, but next time talk to Abby first. There are laws and rules that the business has to follow."

"I understand."

"Good." He smacked Mattie's back and drew the kid in for a hug. "Let's get out of here. We'll visit the shop first and then grab dinner somewhere."

"Tacos?" Mattie hopefully asked.

Jack laughed. "You want me to chase down Thai and Chuy's truck again, don't you?"

"I have an app on my phone." Mattie tapped at the screen. "It tells me where my favorite food trucks are. Kelly's Bee made it."

He smiled at the way Mattie described his brother's girlfriend. To his mind, the ownership in that relationship was totally reversed. It was Bee who had owned Kelly—heart and soul—since she was a teenager. Though they were taking things slowly now and re-building the broken trust that existed between them after that clusterfuck stalker situation, Jack had no concerns about the couple. Given time, their relationship would heal.

As he walked Mattie out of the gym and waved at Finn to let him know that he was heading home for the evening, Jack decided he'd better put some time and effort into the relationship he wanted with Abby. The gym was doing great. His brothers were both in good places. Even Pop was safe and out of trouble for the moment. There might not ever be a more perfect time than this one, and he was grabbing it with both hands and refusing to let go.

Mattie chatted his ear off on the ride to the pawn shop and clued him in on the filthy joke his workout buddies had told. Knowing Abby would flip if she heard Mattie repeat it, he launched into a quick lesson on locker room and boys-only talk. While some people tried to shield Mattie from everything, Jack took the view that Mattie was a grown man with the same interests as every other hot-blooded guy. He just needed to be told in clear-cut language what was and wasn't socially acceptable.

"Is that a boundary, Jack?"

Familiar with the boundaries talks Abby had with her brother, he nodded. "Yes, it's one of those social boundaries that we all have to learn."

"So I can laugh at dirty jokes at the gym?"

"Yes."

"But I can't tell them at the shop?"

"Exactly," he said, hoping to hell Mattie would follow through on the lesson. He found a parking spot in the lot across the street from the pawn store and killed his engine.

"You don't tell dirty stories at the gym, Jack."

"No, I don't."

"Why?"

"Because it's my business and it's unprofessional," he answered matter-of-factly. "It's also juvenile and can be disrespectful, especially toward women."

Mattie unbuckled his seatbelt and seemed to be considering what he had said. "I don't want to be disrespectful." With a broad grin, he reached for his door handle. "And I love women."

"So do I. They deserve to be treated with respect and protected, not talked about in locker rooms, gyms, and man caves, okay?"

"Okay, Jack."

They left the truck and crossed the street. For a Monday evening, the shop seemed to be rather slow. He chalked it up to news of the robbery. By tomorrow night, the place would be teeming with customers. With the current economy and the expenses of a typical summer, people wouldn't stay away long.

When they stepped inside, the chimes sounded nice and loud to alert the floor staff. With the practiced eyes of a Marine, he scanned the shop and instantly detected Abby, the two security guards, her two brokers, and Dan, the night manager. The two employees and Dan were helping customers in different areas of the store. One security guard hovered just to his left watching the door, while another was at the rear of the shop keeping an eye on the customers and transactions. Nothing about them pinged his internal radar, so he moved on to the only person who interested him.

Abby stood at the jewelry counter in her usual outfit of jeans and a bright green polo shirt embroidered with the company logo. Gold and silver chevrons dangled from her ears and glinted every time she moved. She had taken out the braids she had been wearing the last time he had seen her and now had curls spilling around her shoulders.

What he wouldn't give to be able to wake up every morning and nuzzle in close to those dark waves! She would fit perfectly in his arms, her lithe ballerina-like body molded against his heat and strength. Throbbing need uncurled in his stomach at the idea of seeing her smiling face in the early morning sunshine. He doubted there could be anything more beautiful than that.

Tearing his gaze away from the object of his desire, Jack examined the younger guy, probably close to Mattie's age, who had his pants hanging down below his ass and his boxers in full view. Jack zeroed in on the colors of the basketball jersey the guy wore. The little gangster wannabe had one leg bent with his full weight resting on his toes. The easily visible sole of his white sneaker had three hand-drawn numbers marking it.

1-8-7. It was the police code for a homicide and the name of the upstart gang that was trying to make a name for themselves in the area. The youngest, newest members were only allowed to show their affiliation by marking the bottoms of their shoes and wearing the gang's colors. Later, they would earn the rights to tattoos and bolder markings.

Eyes narrowed, Jack carefully watched the interaction. The moment he had heard about the robbery, he had suspected the 1-8-7 crew might be behind it. His second thought? The same Albanian outfit that had caused his family such a headache in early June. Jack would never forgive that bastard Besian for forcing Kelly to fight as his champion in the underground bare-knuckle tournament. Kelly could have been killed by the Russian giant who fought for Russian mob boss Nikolai Kalasnikov—and for what?

Money.

The same thing the guy hassling Abby wanted.

"Look, lady, I'm telling you this is real gold."

"I didn't say it wasn't. I said that all I can do with this is scrap it."

"Scrap? Are you crazy?"

"No, I'm a businesswoman. Do you honestly think I have a line of customers coming into my shop asking for a gold chain that says *PIMP*?" She gave the necklace a jiggle. "If I buy this, it goes into the scrap heap to be melted."

"Baby, you cold."

Jack's fingers curled at his sides. He didn't want anyone calling her baby but him. Holding himself back, he waited to see how she would react. One thing Abby had always made clear was her ability to handle even the toughest situations herself.

Abby cast an annoyed glare at the man. "I'm not your baby. Cut the crap and tell me what you want for all this." She gestured to the pile of jewelry on the counter. "And don't tell me three grand again because that number is a dream."

"Give me fifteen hundred."

She shook her head and poked through the rings and chains. "I'll give you eight."

"Eight! That's robbery."

Abby's lips pursed. "Sir, you came in here to ask me to buy your jewelry. I didn't ask you to come into my shop and cause a ruckus. All right? Now," she blew out a breath and sorted through the jewelry. "I'll give you two for this one, fifty for both of these, two for this one and three for this ring. That's it. Take it or leave it."

"Well I need more than that!"

"If you want to pawn instead of sell, I can go to twelve."

He considered her offer and then reached up to his mouth. He pried free his gold grill and held it out to her. "What about this?"

Abby stared at the slimy jewelry thrust toward her face. "Are you for real? You want me to price your grill?"

"It's gold."

She stared at the item for a few seconds before sliding to the left and crouching down to retrieve a roll of paper towels. After ripping a handful free, she reached out for the grill and wiped it clean. Holding it with another towel, she lifted her jeweler's loupe from the chain around her neck and examined the item. "How much did you pay for this?"

"Two thousand."

She lifted her gaze. "Seriously?"

"Yeah. Why? You gonna tell me those ain't real diamonds or gold now?"

"The diamonds are real," she said, "but they're small. We're talking ten points and low quality." She dropped the loupe and took the grill to the gold testing spot along the counter behind her. With the ease and efficiency of a skilled appraiser, she scraped the metal and dripped nitric acid onto it. "The gold is real but it is 10 carat."

"What? No. No. No. That's 14 carat."

Abby sighed and carried the grill back to the customer. "It's not. It's exactly what I said it is, and the retail value is probably five or six hundred bucks. I'd offer you, like, two hundred if you want to sell and maybe three hundred to loan."

"This is bullshit! You're a thief! Trying to rip me off and take my gold!"

"I'm a thief?" Shaking her head, Abby dropped the grill onto the pile of jewelry. "You know what? Take your stuff and get out of my store."

"I ain't going nowhere, lady. You're gonna give me what I want."

Abby chortled and rolled those gorgeous brown eyes. "Or what?"

"You don't wanna see what I got under here, bitch." That scrawny bastard reached toward the front of his pants, sliding his hand under his shirt.

Seeing red, Jack reacted on instinct. He bolted across the shop, snatched the back of the guy's jersey and jerked him upright. Gripping the little shit's wrist, he dragged it toward the center of his back. A loud *thunk* echoed amid gasps as a wicked looking knife dropped to the floor. Jack kicked it behind him and then smashed the threatening prick's face down against the glass of the jewelry case.

"Man, get off me!"

Dropping his mouth close to the other man's ear, he hissed, "No one talks to Abby that way." He pushed the bastard's thumb back and drew a yowl of pain.

"You're going to take your cheap ass chains and get the hell out of here."

The man slapped at the counter with his free hand and gathered up his goods. Still holding him by the back of the shirt, Jack walked him out of the shop. The security guard closest to the door held it open for him. Jack jerked his head toward the knife on the ground. "Put that away some place safe and call the police."

Out in the night, he dragged the would-be attacker to the corner. Before he let go, he made sure to give the man one final warning. "If I ever see you around here again, I'll rip that nasty grill out of your mouth and shove it up your ass. Understood?"

With a rough shove, he sent the skinny asshole stumbling forward. The kid straightened up and fixed Jack with a menacing stare. "You done made a big mistake, man. Huge!"

A harsh laugh erupted from Jack's throat. "Kid, I lived through two tours in Iraq and another two in Afghanistan. I've been shot. I've been blown up. I've survived a helicopter crash and a firefight. There ain't shit that you and your loser friends can do that scares me."

All bravado fled from the kid's face. Had he finally realized that he was dealing with a different breed of man? Jack meant every word he had said. He didn't make idle threats, not when it came to the safety of the people he cared for most. This prick was lucky he was getting away this easily after trying to hurt Abby.

My Abby. The possessive thought burned through him. It was one he could no longer deny. It was one he was determined to make a reality.

Hitching up his pants, the wannabe gangster pivoted on his heel. Jack watched him walk away until he disappeared around a corner. Heading back into the shop, he discovered Abby in a heated discussion with Dan while Mattie methodically cleaned the smudge created by that jerk's face on the glass case. Not liking the way Dan talked down to Abby, Jack forced his feet to remain frozen to the spot. Abby didn't need him riding to her rescue all the time. She was perfectly capable of handling her employee.

"We'll discuss this tomorrow, Dan. It's been a long day, and we're all on edge."

"It's theft, Abby."

Back ramrod straight, Abby looked like a viper ready to strike. "Are you seriously going to stand there and say that?"

Jack quickly read the situation and realized it was about the watch now tucked into the pocket of his jeans. He quickly ate up the floor with long strides and retrieved the watch. Holding it out, he said, "It wasn't theft. It was an honest mistake. I'm happy to pay for it."

"It's already been paid for," Abby informed him. "I covered the full retail price of the watch we would have assigned to it when it went onto the floor. The shop made plenty of money off this watch." Glancing at Dan, she added, "Which you would have known if you had let me speak to you in the morning."

The older man's ears turned red. "You could have said—"

"I don't have to say anything, Dan. It's my shop. I don't have to clear every single move I make with you." With an irritated huff, she spun away from the night manager and stalked back to her brother.

With his face puffed out and just as red as his ears, Dan muttered under his breath and stormed away to the line of cash registers. Still surprised by that wasp-ish tone Abby had used, Jack slipped the watch back into his pocket and made his way to the jewelry counter Mattie had just finished cleaning. Taking in Abby's tired eyes and tense posture, Jack decided that she needed dinner, a hot bath, and a massage.

"Abby." He spoke firmly but softly. "Get your purse and head home. Mattie and I are going to grab dinner. We'll meet you there."

"Jack, I don't need—"

"You need to get some rest. You need a hot meal and some time to unwind." He cupped her beautiful face with one hand, loving the way her darker skin looked against his tanned fingers, and gently brushed his thumb along the apple of her cheek. Her eyes widened fractionally, and she inhaled a surprised breath. In all the years they had been friends, it was the first time he had ever touched her so intimately.

It wouldn't be the last.

"Let me take care of you tonight."

An expression that seemed suspiciously close to panic crossed her face. "I can take care of myself, Jack."

"I never said you couldn't." He let his thumb trace that pouty lower lip of hers. He wanted nothing more than to dip his head and finally claim her mouth, but this wasn't the time or place. Later, he would get that kiss he wanted so badly. It would be the sort of kiss that left her trembling and panting. "Abby?"

She swallowed hard. "All right. I'll get my stuff and meet you at the house." She glanced back at her brother who looked on curiously. With a slant to her mouth, she added, "I'm sure he's going to make you chase down that taco truck he loves so much, but don't let him bamboozle you into believing that it's okay for him to order that atomic hot sauce. He'll be up all night with heartburn."

Jack smiled. "I'll take that under advisement."

Abby dared to touch his chest. Her small hand felt so damned good rubbing that circle. He wanted to feel her skin against his without the thin cotton barrier between them. "Thank you, Jack. I appreciate you stepping in with that loser."

"He won't bother you again."

"I hope not."

"I'll make sure of it." He had never wanted to draw her close and kiss her forehead more. Fighting the urge to claim her so publicly, he let his hand fall from her face. "Where's the knife?"

"Pete locked it away in the safe and called Santos while you were dragging that guy outside. He'll pick it up in the morning and review the security tapes. He has a feeling he knows who that jerk was."

Jack had always been impressed with the detective and trusted he would handle the problem. "Get your stuff. I'll walk you out to your car."

She nodded, disappeared into the back, and returned with her purse a short time later. He noticed the way she gave Dan a wide berth. He suspected the friction there existed because the older man had expected to take a more prominent role in the business after Mr. Kirkwood had passed. Jack wasn't sure why the man would have thought such a thing. It had been clear to anyone who had known Abby's grandfather that he had always planned for Abby to take his place, just as he had taken his father's in the family business.

With Mattie and Abby in front of him, Jack trailed them outside. He tried to keep his needy gaze from lingering on that fine, taut ass of Abby's, but those jeans she wore were too tempting. Every Wednesday night during his self-defense class, she tormented him in workout pants that hugged her bottom so tightly. More than once, he had been forced to move to the back of the class while the women practiced their moves because Abby caused such a wild response in him.

He made sure Abby got into her car before sliding behind the wheel of his truck. Mattie was already buckled in and tapping at his phone screen, no doubt using that app Bee had created to help him track down the food truck. "Jack?"

"Yeah, bud?" He eased out of the parking space.

"Do you like Abby?"

His gut clenched. *Shit.* What if Mattie didn't approve? "Yeah, I like Abby."

Mattie was silent for a moment so long that Jack's stomach actually pitched with anxiety. "That's good."

Releasing a pent-up breath, he said, "I'm glad you think so. Now—where's this truck?"

Mattie showed him the map and the blinking icon. Jack quickly oriented himself and turned right at the next stoplight. They drove along for another minute or so before Mattie spoke again. "Hey, Jack?"

"Yeah?"

"You owe two dollars to the swear jar now. You said a-s-s."

Remembering some of the language he had used outdoors, Jack laughed. "We better make it five bucks, kid."

3 CHAPTER THREE

Bumping hips with Jack in the kitchen of my childhood home felt so strange, and yet in some way, oddly familiar. Side by side, we arranged the leftovers from our feast of Asian-influenced tacos while Mattie stacked plates and silverware in the already full sink. Our dishwasher had been on the fritz for weeks, but I hadn't had the time to get it repaired. Seeing the stack of dishes waiting for me was yet another reminder that I really needed to get on that.

My fingers brushed against Jack's when we both reached for a container of the crunchy shortbread cookies Mattie loved so much. The accidental touch reminded me of the deliberate and gentle way he had stroked my cheek back at the store. After watching him expertly handle the situation with that knife-wielding nut, I understood that there was a darker, dangerous side to Jack Connolly, one he kept well-hidden.

For me, it seemed he had been willing to unleash that frighteningly skilled beast. I couldn't quite describe the way that made me feel. No man had ever come to my defense like that. Jack's actions made me feel...special.

"It's 9:15," Mattie announced. "I have to go."

I glanced at the clock on the microwave and noticed the late time. My brother stood next to the sink overflowing with dishes and wrung his hands. Knowing only too well how he needed his routines, I smiled and shooed him off. "Go on to bed, Mattie. I'll get the dishes tonight."

He relaxed instantly and leaned over to kiss my cheek. "Night, Abby."

I gave him a quick hug. "Night, Mattie. Make sure you set your alarm and plug in your cell phone to recharge."

"Okay." He grabbed the small container of *polvorones*.

"Don't eat those in bed. You'll get powdered sugar on everything."

He exhaled with frustration at my nagging. "*Okay,* Abs."

I held up both hands. "Sorry."

After grabbing a handful of paper towels to guard against crumbs, Mattie stood in front of Jack with such indecision playing upon his face. Making up his mind, he gave Jack a very manly but less than forceful punch to the arm. "Night, bro."

Jack grinned and clapped Mattie on the back. "Night, bud."

Mattie made it all the way to the arched doorway before he turned back. "Jack, you forgot to put five dollars in the swear jar."

"You're right. I sure did." Jack tugged his wallet from the back pocket of his jeans and retrieved a five dollar bill that he promptly deposited into the swear jar sitting on the counter.

Satisfied that Jack had played by the rules, Mattie left the kitchen. Amused by the way the two men interacted, I shot Jack an appreciative smile. "Thank you."

"For?" He loaded up his arms with the plastic containers of leftovers and carted them to the refrigerator.

"For treating Mattie like any other guy," I explained and opened the icebox for him. "Most people just see his Down Syndrome. Sometimes they treat him in an almost patronizing way. It makes my skin

ROXIE RIVERA

crawl. You don't do that. You treat him like any other younger brother."

"I treat him exactly the way I would want someone to treat Finn or Kelly." Jack closed the refrigerator door. "So 9:15?"

"It's the routine he prefers. He showers, changes into his pajamas, and watches two episodes of his favorite television show. After that, it's his prayers and bed."

"Every night?"

I nodded and moved to the sink. "Every night."

Jack tapped the dishwasher. "What's wrong with this?"

"It stopped rinsing a few weeks ago, but I found a tutorial online that helped me fix that one. Now it won't fill with water at all."

"I'll take a look at it tomorrow afternoon. If that's okay?"

I laughed. "Like I'm going to turn down a free handyman?"

Jack chuckled and pushed his hip against mine. "Scoot down. I'll wash if you'll rinse and dry."

Not at all surprised that he was willing to pitch in, I moved to stand in front of the empty sink and grabbed a dishtowel and sponge from the drawer while Jack rearranged the stacks of dishes, cups, and silverware. When the sink was brimming with sudsy water, he reached for the sponge and got to work.

I couldn't stop staring at those big, strong hands of his. He wasn't as stocky as his youngest brother Kelly, but he was taller and leaner than Finn. Jack had an incredible physique with muscular forearms and biceps that stretched the sleeves of his T-shirts. This close to him, I relished the incredible heat and that intoxicating, woodsy scent that followed him everywhere. It had to be his soap. Jack didn't strike me as the type of guy who misted himself with cologne just to hang around his gym.

Our fingers touched every time he handed me a dish to rinse and dry. I tried to ignore the illicit thrill that sparked deep in my core, but it was impossible. My thoughts kept turning back to the way Jack had so tenderly cupped my face and traced my lip. His action left no chance for misinterpretation. Jack wanted *me*. I didn't know why or even when that had happened, but it was clear as day.

I practically vibrated with giddiness at the discovery. *Me. Me. Me. He wants me.*

"Abs?" He waved a plastic tumbler. "You zoned out there for a second."

"Oh. Sorry." Flushed, I reached for the cup and rinsed it quickly. Trying to get a grip, I searched for a safe discussion topic. My gaze landed on the tattoo marking the underside of his left forearm. It was the first time I had been at the right angle to read the Latin inscription inked on his skin. "Fortune favors the bold, huh?"

Jack glanced at me with surprise. "You know Latin?"

"Catholic school," I explained.

"Really?" He seemed even more surprised by that.

"I went to St. Mary's."

"The private school?"

"I was a scholarship kid." The all-girls academy was the best in Houston and had a rigorous curriculum that sent all of its graduates to good colleges. "Actually, I was in the same class as Lena Cruz. Erin Hanson and Cassie Roberts were in the year below us." Knowing that Jack had recently had trouble with Cassie's boyfriend, John Hagen, I didn't mention the connection. Instead, I asked, "Do you know Erin?"

"Ivan Markovic's new wife?"

"Yep."

"I know her by sight. She's really pretty—and not at all the type of woman I would ever expect a man like Ivan to marry."

"Their wedding was really beautiful. They seem to be madly in love with each other."

"She must love him to take on that history," he muttered. Scrubbing a plate, he asked, "What about Bee Langston and her friends?"

"You mean like Hadley Rivera?"

"The one who draws comics?"

"Graphic novels," I corrected. "She was a year under me and in the same class as Vivian Valero. Er—I guess she's Kalasnikov, now. Bee Langston and her bestie Coby, the DJ, were a year behind those two. Caitlin Weston went to school with us for a while, but she graduated really early, even earlier than Bee. Pips Barlow Bennett, the oil heiress who hangs around with Ty Weston, was in the same year as Lena and Erin too."

"Jesus," Jack breathed with a tinge of awe. "You've just listed the who's who of Houston."

"The program attracts the best. We've all stayed in touch, networked, and supported one another."

"I guess Beyoncé was right about girls owning the world," he said with a playful wink.

I rolled my eyes and flicked suds at him. "I never pegged you as the Beyoncé type."

He splashed me back. "What can I say? I'm a well-rounded guy."

I giggled and dabbed at my cheek with the dish-towel. Looking at the bold ink on his arm, I asked, "So why that motto?"

"It's the way I've lived my life."

"Does that mean you like taking risks?"

"Calculated risks? Sure."

"Like?"

"Like this one." With those lighting reflexes of his, Jack swooped down toward me and planted his lips against mine. Shocked by his unexpected kiss, I inhaled a sharp breath. My eyelashes fluttered together and excitement rocked me. The chaste touch of his lips against mine, an innocent, sweet kiss like two teenagers on a first date might exchange, ended much too soon.

Still reeling from the surprise of it, I blinked and peered up into the grass green eyes that had enthralled me from day one. "Jack?"

"Tell me to stop, Abby. If you don't want me, you need to tell me right now."

I gulped as his roughened voice sent shivers right through me. "And if I do want you?"

His forehead touched mine. "Kiss me, Abby. Show me how much you want me."

Gripping his shirt, I rose on tiptoes and captured the mouth of the man who had been starring in my fantasies for ever so long. Though I initiated the kiss, Jack quickly took control. Something told me that he would always be the one in control, the commanding alpha male who protected and supported me, and I wouldn't have it any other way.

He cradled my face in his wet hands and flicked his tongue against the seam of my lips. I clutched at his arms, desperate for something to hold onto, and let him swipe his tongue across mine. Head pounding, I prayed my shaky legs would hold me up as Jack stabbed deeper and kissed me with such passion.

As if reading my mind, Jack crouched down and used those brawny arms of his to lift me right up. He deposited me on the nearest countertop, and I wrapped my legs around his waist, drawing him in and keeping him close. His strong hands gripped the front of my polo shirt, tugging it free from my jeans, and then slid under the fabric to stroke my bare belly. His fingertips were rough and hot, rasping me and setting me on fire.

"Jack." I breathed his name with such need. I couldn't believe this was happening. It was a million times hotter than I had ever imagined. Nearly delirious with desire, I rocked against Jack and encouraged the exploration of his masterful hands.

He plundered my mouth, taking what he wanted and giving me so much pleasure in return. Clasping my nape, he tilted my head back and gazed down into my eyes. We were both breathing hard now and both desperate for more, so very much more. "Abby, I want—"

But he didn't get the rest of that thought finished.

A terrifying crash shattered our beautiful moment. Squealing tires and exploding glass could be heard throughout the house.

Jack snatched me right off the counter, dragged me down to the floor, and covered my body with his. As if he had never left the battlefield, he shouted orders to Mattie, commanding him to stay put and lock his bedroom door. Pushing me into a corner where I would be well protected, he pinned me with a stern, no-nonsense look as he fished his cell phone from his jeans. Shoving it into my hand, he said, "Stay here. Call 9-1-1. Do not come after me. Understand?"

"Yes, Jack."

He kissed my forehead and rushed out of the kitchen. Dialing the phone with shaking fingers, I prayed he would come back to me in one piece.

With a calm learned through many years in combat, Jack crept into the living room and killed the light by smacking the nearest switch. The room was plunged into darkness. Without the light silhouetting him, he was no longer an easy target. Though he had heard the squeal of tires following that explosion of glass, he didn't dare trust the miscreants who had attacked Abby's home to leave so easily.

Enough moonlight illuminated the space to let him see what had happened. Warm, muggy air drifted into the living room through a broken window. The slats of the wooden blinds were cracked and hanging awkward-ly. As he hugged the wall and cautiously moved to-ward the front door, planting each footstep deliberately down on the hickory planks, Jack spotted the heavy brick sitting in the center of the room.

His gut lurched when he considered how badly that brick could have hurt Mattie or Abby if they had been sitting in the living room watching television as so many people did this time of night. He refused to even think about how lucky they were that it had only been a brick and not gunfire. He couldn't even stomach the thought of either of them being seriously injured.

Listening intently and scoping out the quiet street, he confirmed it was safe to venture outside. The neighbors to the left were coming out of their front door, one of them on his cell phone and rattling off his address to the police. Sirens were already wailing in the distance and growing louder. He wasn't surprised by the quick response.

Though Abby and Mattie lived on one of the safer streets in this neighborhood, the area still had a bad reputation for violence and crime despite the efforts of the community to tamp it down. Judging by the speed of the response, a unit had been patrolling very near. Hopefully someone had seen the car that had brought the vandals to Abby's front door. Whether they would talk was another issue altogether.

Back in the house, he quickly returned to Abby and found her exactly where he had left her. She flung herself at him, wrapping her arms around his neck and letting him drag her into his embrace. He kissed the side of her neck and rubbed a reassuring hand down her back. "It's okay, sweetness. We're all right. It was only a brick."

"A brick? Why? Who would do something like that?"

Jack had a good idea and lowered her until her feet touched the floor. "Maybe that punk who tried to pull a knife on you in the store."

She continued to lean against him. "You really think he would take it that far?"

"I do." He heard a noise that sounded like Mattie's voice and grasped her hand. "Let's get Mattie. The police will be here any second, and he's going to be scared."

With their fingers interlaced, they made their way across the modestly-sized ranch-style house to Mattie's bedroom. The younger man sat wide-eyed on his bed and hugged his knees. Abby started to rush toward him, but Jack stopped her. He took the lead this time, certain Mattie didn't need or want to be coddled.

"Hey, bud, it's okay." He crouched down in front of the bed and tapped Mattie's knee. "Some bad guys tossed a brick through the window, but they're gone now. The cops are here, and we're all okay. Everyone is safe."

Mattie took it all in and finally nodded. "Okay, Jack—but it was *really* loud."

"I know it was." He motioned toward the television. "You want to keep watching your shows or do you want to come with us to talk to the police?"

Mattie shook his head. "I need to watch my shows. I've already seen the police before and they're not as cool as the firemen."

Jack smiled. "No, I guess not."

He stepped back to let Abby give her brother a hug and noticed the irritated expression on her face. The pinched set to her lips didn't bode well for him, and he accurately guessed he had overstepped the line by going to comfort Mattie first. Out in the hallway, she waited until the door was shut behind her to frown at him. "Why did you do that?"

"I knew what he needed. You're tense with fear and anxiety. I wanted him to see me and know that I have it under control."

"You're acting like I'm hysterical."

"Sugar, you're getting there," he said gently and reached for her trembling hand. A short while ago, she had been trembling for a totally different reason. Now she shook with terror and adrenaline.

Abby let him tug her close but she didn't allow him to pull her into his embrace. She tipped back her head and stared up at him with a bit of warning reflecting in those chocolate-brown eyes. "Jack, I'm his sister. *I* know what he needs."

Remembering what she had said earlier, he reminded her, "You told me that you appreciate the way I treat him like any other twenty-year-old man. That's what I was doing, Abby."

She considered his statement. Finally, she admitted, "It's hard for me to let someone else in, Jack. For years, I was all Mattie had. Until Granddad rescued us from that roach-infested hellhole where our mother kept us, it was just me and Mattie. That's it."

Jack wrapped his arms around Abby and hauled her in tight. His stomach pitched at the image of a tiny Abby shielding her baby brother in such an awful place. He had known that their mother had been a drug addict but he hadn't had any idea it was *that* bad. He pressed his lips to her temple and let them linger. "I'm used to being in charge, Abby. I've always been that way, even as a kid. I may have left my career as an officer in the Marine Corps behind, but I'm still that same man."

"I like that man," she admitted quietly. "He makes me feel safe."

Eyes closing briefly, Jack relished her admission. "I won't let anyone hurt you or Mattie. I swear it, Abby."

She leaned back and smiled up at him. "I've never doubted that, Jack."

A knock at the door interrupted their tender moment. Taking her hand, Jack headed for the door and opened it to reveal a pair of police officers standing on the front porch. After giving his statement, Jack retrieved his phone from Abby's hand and called Finn while she talked to the police about the break-in at her shop, the run-in with the gang member, and now this brick incident.

"Hey, bro," Finn greeted cheerfully. "Where are you? We're about to start a new round of Trivial Pursuit. Bee and Kelly are crushing Pop and me."

Considering Bee's brilliant mind that didn't surprise him in the least. "Finn, leave Pop with Bee. Get Kelly and meet me at Abby's place."

"What's wrong?" Finn's tone instantly changed. "Are you okay? Is Abby okay? What about Mattie?"

"We're okay, but we need some plywood or plastic sheeting. Some asshole threw a brick through a window."

"What's going on?" Kelly's deep voice rumbled in the background.

"Someone tried to hurt Abby and Mattie," Finn answered.

"Son of a bitch," Kelly grumbled. "Tell Jack we're on our way."

"I'm sure he heard you," Finn said. "Hell, I'm sure half of Houston heard you bellowing like that."

Shaking his head at his younger brothers, Jack interrupted their squabbling. "Finn, today would be nice."

"Yeah. We're coming. See you soon."

Glad to have his brothers on their way, Jack put away his phone and returned to Abby's side. By now, another familiar face had arrived on the scene. Looking tired as hell but fully focused on the crime, Detective Eric Santos listened intently to Abby's recollection of the events before conferring with the patrolmen who would be handling the case.

After making it clear he wanted to be kept in the loop, Eric caught Jack's eye and motioned with his fingers. Jack trailed the detective to a more private spot away from the officers and Abby. Eric ran his fingers through his midnight black hair and sighed. "I worried something like this would happen."

"I'm sure it was that asshole who tried to get nasty with Abby in her store. Only a coward throws a brick through a damned window."

"Agreed," Eric replied. Forehead creased with concern, the detective confessed, "When I heard the call go out for Abby's house, I thought for sure it was a drive-by. I couldn't get here fast enough."

Jack considered the detective's concern for Abby and Mattie a testament to the other man's character. "Mattie wanted to stay inside, but you might pop in to see him before you go. He was pretty rattled."

"And Abby?" Eric eyed her for a moment. "She might fool other people with that calm, cool exterior but not me. I've known her too long for that."

Not for the first time, Jack wondered if there wasn't something more to the friendship and history between the pair. "I've got it under control."

Eric's eyebrows arched at his possessive tone. "So you finally worked up the courage to stake your claim?"

Jack's eyes narrowed. "Was it that obvious?"

The detective snorted. "You went behind my back to bribe the summer league coordinator to put Mattie on your team. I wouldn't be much of a detective if I didn't put two-and-two together."

"It wasn't like that," Jack grumbled.

Eric snorted. "Yeah, man. Sure it wasn't." Growing serious, he said "Listen, this brick thing? It's probably a one-and-done deal. The 1-8-7 crew knows better than to push too hard with Abby."

"I hope that's true. I keep telling myself she's respected in the community, and her shop helps lots of people. They don't need that kind of backlash."

"True, but it's more than that." Eric hesitated. "You need to talk to Abby about her connection to Besian Beciraj."

Jack's jaw tightened when the name of the Albanian mob boss who had put his family through hell only a few short weeks ago registered. He glanced at Abby, who was talking to her neighbors. He refused to believe that she could be involved in any dirty dealings. She wasn't that sort of woman.

Was she?

"I've got to run, Jack. Should I put a car on the house or—"

"I'm staying," he interjected. "I'm not leaving Abby alone at night until this mess is cleared up."

"I'm glad to hear that." Eric smacked his arm. "Don't hesitate to call me. I'm always available for my friends. Tell Mattie I'll touch base with him tomorrow and see if he'd like to go out for a bite later this week."

"Will do."

Jack returned to Abby's side and put a reassuring hand on her shoulder. She smiled up at him and continued on with her conversation. Once the neighbors and police were gone, Jack followed her back inside the house. While she checked in on Mattie, he grabbed a broom and dustpan and got to work. The brick had been taken away by the police as evidence, but the mess remained.

He was scooping up glass shards when Kelly and Finn arrived. His youngest brother had a toolbox and slab of plywood from the scrap collection in the garage at the house they shared. Finn carried a small overnight bag and a tarp. Eyes narrowed and jaws clenched, they surveyed the damage.

Finally, Finn spoke. "Our fix won't be pretty, but it will do until morning." He lifted the overnight bag. "I packed your things. I figured you'd be staying here tonight." Lowering his voice, he dropped the small piece of luggage on the nearest chair. "Make sure you keep that away from Mattie—if you know what I mean."

Jack got the message loud and clear. Mattie's curiosity could make for a dangerous situation if he started going through the bag and discovered a handgun and ammo. "Understood."

"Oh! Hey." Abby reacted with surprise upon finding his brothers in her living room. Her gaze flitted to the tools and supplies. "Wow. Thanks. That's really nice of you two to come over so late to help."

"We're happy to do it," Finn assured her.

"We'll be out of your hair in no time," Kelly promised and got to work.

Jack stepped closer to Abby and brushed his knuckles down her cheek. "Is Mattie all right?"

"He's already fast asleep." She leaned into his touch and smiled up at him. "I guess you were right about how to deal with him." Inhaling a long breath, she said, "If you don't need my help, I'll go finish up those dishes."

"We've got this covered."

She nodded and left his side, her slow movements showing her reluctance. He sensed she was beginning to feel the crash from the fight-or-flight response that had kicked in when the brick had come through the window. As soon as the repairs were complete, he would make sure she got the attention she needed.

"So whose ass are we kicking?" Kelly asked as he held up one side of the plywood while Finn hammered nails in place.

Jack readjusted his side of the plywood slab so it completely covered the shattered window. "We aren't kicking any asses just yet. This is a tangled mess, and I need to know all the angles before we act. We can't do anything that would put Abby or Mattie at risk."

"You think this is tied in with the robbery at her store?" Finn asked as he gingerly stepped around the flowers planted in the bed beneath the window.

Jack shook his head. "This was personal. That robbery wasn't."

"What did they take?"

"Video cameras, cell phones, and cameras," Jack said. "Abby told me that nothing else was touched, not the jewelry or guns or knives."

"That's weird."

Jack thought it was more than weird. "It feels calculated. Someone wanted those items for a very specific reason."

"Maybe it's a situation like the one with Bee," Kelly suggested. "Someone got a hold of those pictures of Jeb and used them to blackmail and extort her. Maybe someone pawned a device with sensitive photos on it. If you wanted it back, you would steal everything to provide some cover for your actions."

It was a possibility Jack hadn't considered. "If that's the case, I hope it was only someone trying to get back evidence of an affair or a sex tape and not an even worse crime."

"My advice?" Finn finished hammering the final nail. "Tell Abby to let it go. File her police report. File with the insurance. Leave it at that. If someone was willing to break into a business to get back a phone or a video camera, they're committed. She doesn't need that sort of trouble."

As usual, Finn offered sound advice. "I'll talk to her. You got a tape measure in that tool box?"

"Yep." Finn found the item in question, a notepad, and pencil. They measured the window and Jack jotted down the numbers.

"Leave the tool box," he said as Kelly tidied up the area. "I need to take a look at the dishwasher."

"Figure out what you need and text me the info." Kelly stepped back to examine the plywood. "I'll head in to the hardware store first thing in the morning. Pop needs to get out and walk around some. I'll take him with me."

Jack considered his youngest brother for a moment. Since the fight and the shooting that had nearly killed their father, Kelly hadn't reported to work at the private security firm where he worked. "When are you going back to Lone Star?"

Kelly shrugged and tucked the hammer into the toolbox. "I'm not sure."

Jack's eyebrow raised and he shot a look at Finn. "You are planning to go back to work sometime?"

"Maybe," Kelly answered. "While I've been healing up from the tournament and taking care of Pop, I've been doing a lot of thinking."

"About?"

"About what I want out of life," he said matter-of-factly. "Since the day I graduated high school and shipped off to boot camp, I've been putting my life on the line for someone else. Maybe it's time I put me and the people who mean the most to me first."

"You mean Bee," Jack guessed.

"Yes. I nearly lost her. I realize how lucky I am that she gave me a second chance to fix things and make them right between us. She's it for me, Jack. She the one. She's the woman I'm going to marry someday. Right now? She needs me *here*. That's right where I plan to be."

Pride welled upside him. He reached out and tousled Kelly's short hair. "Listen to you! Talking like a big boy!"

Kelly smacked away his hand but couldn't stop the grin that tugged at his mouth. "Screw you."

Finn joined his laughter, but Jack could tell he was equally as proud of their younger brother for growing up and doing right by Bee. Her career was about to skyrocket, and she needed the full support of her man. It was good that Kelly was willing to take time off and commit totally to her.

When his brothers were gone and he was satisfied with the patch job they had done on the window, Jack locked the front door and grabbed his bag. He ducked into the kitchen, but Abby had already finished her chore. Heading down the hallway, he checked on Mattie who slept peacefully before continuing his search for Abby.

The room next to Mattie's had a locked door. He assumed it had belonged to their grandfather and left it alone. The door across the hall was slightly ajar. He heard the sound of rustling fabric and knocked softly. "Abby? May I come inside?"

"Yes."

He pushed open the door and stepped inside her bedroom. The serene space felt instantly relaxing with its soft gray walls and crisp white bedding. Dressed in tiny shorts and a tank top, she displayed inch after tantalizing inch of her trim legs. His tastes had always run to thicker, more voluptuous women, but there was just something about Abby and that perky dancer's frame that revved his engine.

The dimmed bedside lamps cast a warm glow to her rich, dark skin. His fingers just itched to get on her, to glide along her calves and up her thighs. He wanted to peel away those clothes and feel her naked beneath him while he worshipped her with his hands and mouth. He couldn't wait for his chance to pin her down and slide his tongue between the delicate petals of her pussy. He would have her screaming his name in no time.

Shaking himself from those tempting thoughts, he said, "We have the window boarded up for the night. Kelly offered to hit up the hardware store in the morning. If you don't mind, I'll keep Mattie with me so he can help us get the window replaced and fix the dishwasher."

"Are you sure? He can be difficult when it comes to tasks like that."

"I'm a patient man." He needed her to know that he was up for the challenge and in this for the long-haul. "Mattie likes hands-on work. I'm sure he'll love getting his hands dirty and learning some new skills."

"He will." She pinched the front of her shirt and rubbed the cotton between her fingers. The vulnerability reflected on her sweet face hit him right in the gut. "You're staying, right?"

"I'm staying." Dropping his bag, he crossed the space between them and dragged her into his arms. He sat down on the edge of her bed and tugged her between this legs. She perched on his thigh, and he wrapped his arms around her, cocooning her in place and sharing his heat with her. "I'll keep you safe, Abby."

She clutched at his shirt and nuzzled into him. "I keep thinking about what happened. I know they wouldn't have stopped with a brick if your truck hadn't been parked in the driveway."

He had been thinking the same thing but didn't want to frighten her by confirming it. Instead, he kissed her long and slow and deep. When he felt the tension leaving her body, he eased off and peered into her eyes. "I'm here now. I'm not going anywhere. No one will hurt you or Mattie."

She let loose a relaxed sigh and snuggled into him a little more. Detective Santos' instruction to ask Abby about her relationship with the Albanian mob boss ricocheted around his head, but he didn't think this was the right time. After such an incredibly long and stressful day, she needed to rest. Tomorrow he would get the truth out of her.

"If you'll let me borrow a pillow, I'll set up on the couch in the living room."

Her fingers tightened around the fistful of his shirt that she held. "No. I..." Her voice trailed off, but he didn't push her. She had to be the one to ask. Running her finger along the collar of his shirt, she eventually worked up the courage. "Will you stay with me tonight?"

He tipped her chin with his fingers and traced her full lower lip. Grinning, he said, "Try and get rid of me."

She issued a sarcastic snort. "Once you get a good look at the whole package that comes with Miss Abby

Kirkwood, you'll probably go diving out that broken window."

She said it in a way that told him every other man she had dated had done the exact same thing. "Abby, I've been friends with you for quite a while now. I'm fully aware of the dynamics. I won't sit here and say that I understand what it's like to be a twenty-four-seven caregiver and guardian to a special needs adult, but I know what it's like to sacrifice for family. I understand that dating might be tricky."

"Tricky? Jack, it's a minefield."

The imagery that word evoked was too harsh and too violent for the lighthearted way she had used it. Memories of the IED that had claimed Finn's leg and the one that had nearly killed him a few months later blasted him. The chaos, the pain, the panic—it all came flooding back to him. He tried not to show how it affected him, but Abby caught the small flinch and wince.

"Oh God! Jack! I'm so sorry. I didn't mean—ugh. That was really stupid of me."

"Stop." He admonished her firmly but gently. "You don't have to walk around on eggshells around me." He cupped her face. "Baby, we've both got baggage. It's been four years since I left the Corps, and I still have nights where I can't sleep, where I just sit in front of the television and play an endless loop of my deployments in my head."

She pressed her lips to his cheek. "You're the strongest man I've ever known—and I don't mean physically. Everything you've been through and everything you've accomplished? It's amazing, Jack. When I see what you've done for your brothers and your dad, I'm just blown away by you."

He swallowed nervously. Receiving praise had always been an uncomfortable exercise for him. He deflected his discomfort by turning the praise around on her. "You're the amazing one. After everything your mother did, you're still filled with such kindness. The unconditional love you show Mattie and the way you defend and support him and fight for him to have every opportunity he deserves? That's what makes me lo—care for you so much."

At the very last possible instant, he caught himself before blundering into a full accounting of just how much she meant to him. The way Abby made him feel couldn't be denied. When she was near, his heart raced, his palms tingled, and his body thrummed with such excitement. One smile from her, and he felt as if he could slay dragons.

But it was too soon and too new to tell her all that. He had only just worked up the courage to kiss her. She needed time to get used to their friendship chang-

ing from *just friends* to *us* before he confessed that he
had been pining over her for years. And that's where it
was heading. Just as Kelly had started making plans
for his future with Bee, Jack had hopes for a bright,
happy future with Abby.

Come hell or high water, Jack intended to keep her
right where she was—safe in his arms.

4 Chapter Four

"Abby?"

"Yep?" I glanced up from my paperwork to find Marley, one of my part-time pawn brokers, leaning against the door frame of my office. The women's studies student was one of my hardest workers and had been here since she was in high school. She was one of those employees I could count on without question, and I absolutely adored her.

"Mr. Beciraj is here." She pronounced his name with a full Texas twang—*beecher-eye*—and put emphasis on all the wrong syllables. "He says he'd like to speak with you."

I set aside my insurance forms and followed Marley back to the sales floor. I spotted Besian loitering near the jewelry counter but didn't immediately join him. A customer hassling another broker in the luxury goods section caught my eye.

Sizing up the woman, I made my way behind the counter. Though her designer clothing and shoes screamed money, the way she clutched the fur coat with fingers decked out in expensive gold and platinum betrayed her desperation. There was bound to be quite a story to this one.

Catching Mark's gaze, I smiled and slid into the transaction. I held out my hand and greeted the woman. "Hi, I'm Abby Kirkwood, the owner of the shop. Is there something I can do to help you?"

Not making a move to shake my hand or remove her tortoiseshell sunglasses, she blew out an annoyed breath. Her lips hardly twitched, and there was very little movement to her cheeks. Apparently, she was quite a fan of her plastic surgeon. "He's saying that I can't pawn this coat, but it's chinchilla. Surely, you understand what that means."

I didn't let her testy tone bother me. People with money problems weren't really pissed at me. They were pissed at themselves. "It is a gorgeous coat." I ran my fingers along the fur, taking in the silvery, silky guard hair and thick underfur. "Unfortunately, we don't sell very many of these."

"But it's chinchilla," she said, seemingly stuck on the fact that it was one of the finest, rarest furs on the market. "It's worth thousands of dollars."

"Easily," I agreed. "The problem, ma'am, is that it's almost July. In Texas," I added. "It was nearly ninety degrees when I stepped out the front door this morning. No one is buying fur coats right now."

Instead of lashing out as I had expected, the woman crumpled right in front of me. She pushed her sunglasses to the crown of her head, the dark shade of them contrasting starkly with her white-blonde hair. Her red-rimmed eyes were slightly puffy from crying.

"Please," she said finally. "My housekeeper said you're the fairest shop in Houston. I need help. My husband's company is being investigated. They've tied up our assets, and now everyone is suing us. My husband is sick—and they just canceled our insurance. I need cash. Fast."

I studied her face for a long moment. Some people came in here with fake sob stories to try to get one over on the shop, but I could tell this woman was at the end of her rope. One good tug, and she was going to tumble over the edge.

Deciding to help her, I put it out there in black and white. "I won't buy the coat, but I know a lady who runs a luxury goods boutique. She has an online component to her business so she's more likely to take a chance on something like this." I snatched one of our cards from the holder on the counter and tugged free the pen I kept tucked behind my ear at work. "Here's her information. Tell her I sent you. She'll treat you right."

The woman accepted the card. "Thank you."

Looking at her jewelry, I said, "If you want, I can appraise the rings and bracelets you're wearing today and offer you a fair price. We can pawn or sell."

She considered her hands with an almost mercenary glint. Piece by piece, she peeled off the ones she was willing to part with and said, "I'd be willing to sell these."

I took my time appraising the small cache. Everything was top quality and much loved considering the careful care that had been taken of them. Because it was such a large amount of money, I wrote the number on a notepad and slipped it across the counter to her. Poker face in place, the woman stared at it without showing an ounce of emotion. Finally, she nodded. "I'll take it."

"Fantastic." I handed off the items and the slip of paper to Mark. "My associate here will write this up and get you situated." I glanced at him. "Make sure we have one of our security guys walk her out to her car."

"Will do, boss."

"It was a pleasure doing business with you." I extended my hand, and this time she shook it.

"Thank you."

The situation resolved, I joined Besian, who now leaned back against the jewelry counter and watched the bustling store. I noticed his gaze seemed zeroed in on the electronics department. My lips thinned with displeasure when I realized he wasn't staring at the televisions and game systems. No, his intense stare was fixed on Marley.

"You in the market for a new PSP?"

Besian slowly averted his gaze and smiled at me. Tall and lean like Jack, he had dark hair and even darker eyes, the irises nearly as black as his pupils. A long, thin scar bisected his left cheek. A matching scar followed the curve of his throat. I had always wanted to ask him how he had gotten those but didn't dare. I had a feeling it was a story I didn't want to hear.

Though he had only shown me kindness in all the many years he had been a fixture in my life, I held no illusions about him. Besian was one of the most dangerous and powerful men in Houston, second only to reputed mob boss Nikolai Kalasnikov. Considering the way that Russian had made a fortune with his many business interests, I wondered if the real hierarchy was a bit different these days. Nikolai might be the most powerful, but Besian was probably the most dangerous. With a snap of this fingers, he could cause serious pain and trouble for me.

"No, but I see something that would be far more entertaining."

"Don't even think about it."

He seemed amused by my presumption to tell him what to do. "She's an adult. I'm sure we could have fun together."

"She's one of my girls, and—"

"One of your girls, huh? Careful," he said with a sardonic laugh. "You're starting to sound like me."

My lips pursed. "Your girls are strippers—"

"Entertainers," he cut in smoothly.

I rolled my eyes. "You know what I mean. My girls at the shop are good girls who work hard, go to school, and want to build successful lives. They're not doing nasty stuff on a stage to milk some poor loser for a couple of bucks."

"That's not very feminist of you." He had a teasing smile playing upon his mouth. "My girls are hard workers. Many of them are also university students. They're all trying to get into better situations. What you see as a degradation, they see as an opportunity."

Neatly put in my place, I wondered at this defensive side to the Albanian gangster. "So what? You're a champion of women's rights now?"

"I'm a lot of things, sweetheart. If you had taken me up on my invitations for dinner, you would know that."

I pinned him in place with a look. "Not happening."

He held up a hand. "Don't worry. I've heard that you're Jack Connolly's girl now."

A thrill zinged through me at the way he described me as Jack's girl. Last night, after all the fuss had died down, we had slid into bed together. True to his gentlemanly nature, Jack hadn't tried to make even the tiniest move. Other than a sweet and tender good night kiss, nothing else had happened between us. Yet, somehow sleeping so tightly wrapped up in his arms felt more intimate than anything I had ever shared with another man.

Considering how tight-lipped I was about my personal life, I asked, "Do I even want to know where you heard that?"

He shrugged, the fabric of his stone-colored suit jacket stretching easily along his shoulders. Like the woman who had just hocked her jewelry, Besian dressed in exquisitely tailored suits from the best designers. How he afforded that type of wardrobe was another discussion altogether. "When I heard about the robbery, I decided to keep an eye on you. I was told that Jack stayed at your house last night."

I was straight-up irked by the thought of a bunch of gangsters following me. "I don't need you and your guys creeping around my place, Besian."

"Not even after that brick went through your front window?"

I narrowed my eyes. "You know who it was, don't you?"

"Of course, I know. I know everything that goes on in this town."

I waited for him to give me the names of the punks who had vandalized my house. When he didn't volunteer the information, I held out my hands. "Well?"

"Well what?" he asked in that maddeningly calm and cool way.

"Are you going to tell me who it was?"

"You know who it was." He threw up the gang sign of the 1-8-7 crew, and I noticed the fresh scrapes and bruises on his knuckles. As if noticing my stare, he nodded. "It's been taken care of, Abby. You won't have problems like that again."

"Just like that, huh?"

"Consider it a favor."

"I'm not sure you're the sort of man I want to owe a favor."

To his credit, he didn't take offense. Instead, he cracked a smile. "That's because you're a smart woman." With a wave of his hand, he dismissed my concerns. "It's about protecting *my* business interests. I can't have that crew running wild in my backyard. They have to learn to behave themselves—or else."

It was the *or else* part that scared me. Besian wasn't the type of guy who would give someone a stern lecture. He was the type of guy who broke knees...or worse.

"Listen," he stepped closer, close enough that I caught sight of the thin gold chain just barely peeking out from the unbuttoned top of his dress shirt, "I don't like getting involved in other people's business—"

I couldn't help myself. I actually chortled. "Yeah. Sure you don't."

"Ha-ha," he said drily. "What I was trying to say before you interrupted me is that you need to take a closer look at your night manager Dan."

I frowned. "Why?"

"Let's just say that he isn't as squeaky clean as he would like you to believe."

"Bull," I replied forcefully. "That guy has been here forever. He and I don't always see eye-to-eye, but he's a good man."

"I'm sure he is, but that son of his?"

I didn't know much about Leonard. "He's working on a pharmacy degree. From what I know, he's a good student."

Besian's expression turned unreadable. "You should ask Dan about Flea."

The mention of our resident crackhead concerned me. "Flea hasn't been allowed to come on the premises since he tried to sell me that leaf blower and weed eater he stole straight off a landscaping job happening down the street. The damned thing was literally hot when it landed on my counter!"

Besian quirked a smile at my description of that run-in. "He's not allowed on the premises when you're here, but what about at night when Dan is in charge?"

I shook my head. "I check the security tapes every morning. There are two security guys on the night shift. They would tell me if Flea was hanging around this place."

"Hey," Besian said with a light bounce of his shoulders, "it's your business. I thought you might appreciate a heads-up, especially after that break-in."

Signaling an end to our unsettling conversation, he pushed up his cuff and peered at his watch. Unable to help myself, I mentally appraised the luxury timepiece with the rose gold accents and brown crocodile strap. He must have seen my interested gaze because he just chuckled and said, "Sorry, but forty percent of retail is a bit too steep of a discount for me."

"Never say never," I said, thinking of the high-end clients who snuck in here late at night to pawn their family heirlooms just to make the lease payments on their Mercedes or the mortgages on their six bedroom mansions in Royal Oaks.

"Truer words, huh?" Smiling, he backed away and started toward the door. "Tell Jack I said hi."

That was absolutely the last thing I was going to do. Though neither side had confirmed the rumors to me, I had heard all about that scrape between Nick Connolly, Besian, and John Hagen a few weeks earlier. The bruises covering Kelly's battered body had told me all I need to know.

On his way out the door, Besian made a point of catching Marley's gaze. To her credit, she simply frowned at him and got back to work. He didn't seem the least bit deterred and that worried me. The last thing that girl needed was a man like Besian Beciraj sniffing around and wreaking havoc with her carefully laid plans. With a biological dad locked up in the pen and a stepdad who was the vice president of an outlaw motorcycle crew, she had more than enough man trouble in her life.

Ignoring the mobster's interest, she turned her attention to the notepad and game system in front of her. Something about her perplexed expression left me uneasy. I crossed the store and joined her behind the counter. Voice soft, I asked, "Is there a problem?"

"I'm not sure, Abby. Look at this barcode." She showed me the smudged code on the bottom of the game system. "Yesterday, Mattie and I were going through the inventory out here as part of the post-robbery audit. He noticed some of these barcodes were smudged so I had him copy down the serial numbers and descriptions so I could manually compare them with the system."

My brother's big, loopy handwriting made me smile. At some point, he had gotten bored while doing the inventory because he had decorated the margins of the paper with drawings of robots and gigantic dinosaur-like monsters. Apparently he had been learning quite a bit of technique during his sketching classes with Hadley at the arts center she had founded earlier in the year.

"What did you find during your manual search?"

Marley looked around nervously before sliding closer and whispering, "These barcodes belong to products we've already sold. The serial numbers are in the system, but they weren't cross-referenced with the stolen property lists or submitted for verification."

My stomach dropped. "How many of these smudged barcodes did you find?"

"In this section?"

Now my heart raced. "This is happening in other sections of the store?"

She nodded. "I found two watches, a couple of diamond bracelets, six televisions, a couple of DVD players, a stereo, two—"

"Stop," I said, holding up my hand. As the panic subsided, anger overwhelmed me. "Who did the intake for these items?"

Marley hesitated. "Dan."

Suddenly, Besian's warning sounded awfully prescient. "Pull everything with a smudged tag and take it back to the storeroom. I'm not leaving until I figure this out."

Fighting the feelings of betrayal that surged through me, I grabbed the game system and strode back to my office. If what Marley suspected turned out to be true and the store had been put at risk of being closed down for selling stolen property, there was going to be hell to pay.

And I would be starting with Dan.

"Mattie, you almost done packing?" Jack closed the newly repaired dishwasher and scrubbed his hands in the sink. He was drying them when Mattie appeared with his suitcase and collection of DVDs. "You got everything you need?"

"Yes."

Feeling a bit guilty for arranging the sleepover with Finn, Jack wanted to make sure Mattie was fully onboard. Although he had a raging need to be alone with Abby so they could discuss the unexpectedly swift change in their relationship, he refused to do anything that would hurt Mattie's feelings or their friendship. "Are you sure you're okay hanging out with Finn tonight?"

"Jack," he said with a huff, "you've asked me four times. I said yes. I mean yes."

"Okay. I didn't want you to feel pressured."

Mattie rolled his eyes and let loose another exaggerated sigh. "I'm a man of my word, Jack."

He grinned. "Yes, you are."

"Are we going now?"

"Yeah. Let's lock up, and we'll get out of here."

A short time later, Mattie was happily helping Finn tidy up the weights and start the evening laundry loads. Not for the first time, Jack found himself wondering if Mattie would enjoy taking a part-time job at the gym. They had been talking about bringing on an employee to handle some of the everyday tasks that often got pushed aside to deal with clients. Mattie loved the atmosphere at the gym and was always pitching in, even taking the initiative to put together a sign-in sheet for the stations that had the most use so there weren't any more arguments about the gym's standing first-come-first-serve rule.

He was still mulling over the possibility when he arrived at the pawn shop. Sliding out of his front seat, Jack took a moment to enjoy the Texas sunset. The high-rise buildings on the horizon were silhouetted against a sky splashed with vibrant citrus shades. The sight of so much color took him back to the sunsets in Afghanistan. Despite the violence and horror that had marred his tours there, he would always remember the stark beauty of the place.

When he stepped inside the shop, Jack nodded at the security guard near the door. The bulky beast of a man motioned toward the back of the store. "The boss is in the back." He hesitated. "It's tense back there right now. You might be better off waiting for Abby out here."

Jack didn't like the sound of that. Wondering what sort of trouble she had run into now, he crossed the store, weaving in and out of the clumps of customers eyeing merchandise. Mark noticed him approaching the employee only area cordoned off by waist-high counters topped with bullet proof glass. Three lines of customers with tickets in hand waited to pawn, redeem, and sell their items. Their gazes locked and the former Navy pilot reached under the counter to unlock the door. Jack returned the man's wave with an appreciative nod.

Before he even reached the storeroom at the rear of the shop, Jack picked up the sound of raised, angry voices. He easily separated Abby's voice from Dan's. She sounded hurt and betrayed while Dan shouted back in defiant defense.

"I could be arrested, Dan! They could pick me up right now on charges for selling stolen property!"

Jack's eyes widened at Abby's panicked outburst. *What the fuck?*

He stepped forward and twisted the door handle. Thankfully it was unlocked. Otherwise he would have beat on it until one of them let him inside.

"What?" Abby shrieked at him before she realized who it was. Instantly, her angry expression changed to one of sheer embarrassment. "I'm sorry, Jack. I didn't realize—"

"What the hell is going on in here?" He shut the door behind him and blocked Dan's exit, just in case the older man had any funny ideas. "What stolen property, Abby?"

She glanced at Dan, his expression pale and stricken. He skin was nearly as white as his hair now. Whatever was happening here, it was clear he was the guilty party. "It's pawn shop business, Jack. Please let me handle it."

He started to tell her that anything that hurt her was his business but bit his tongue. How would he feel if she barged in on an argument he was having with Finn over the gym? He would be annoyed. Though his instinct was to stay with her and show that she had him standing strong and tall in her corner, he understood that this was something she could handle all on her own.

Pushing off the door, he reached for the handle. "I'll be in the hall."

Abby trailed her soft fingertips down his arm. She offered a pleased smile. "Thank you."

With a stiff nod, he slipped into the hallway and leaned against the wall there. Eyes closed, he concentrated only on the conversation happening on the other side of that door. He tried not to let his thoughts wander ahead of him, but it was difficult to keep them reined in tight. Was this the real reason for the robbery? Was someone trying to get back stolen property that had been fenced? Was it evidence in a crime?

"Why, Dan? Why would you risk *everything* to buy shit off Flea?"

Jack's lips settled into a grim line at the mention of the shifty-eyed and pock-faced junkie Finn jokingly referred to as the neighborhood mascot. The once-promising college athlete had tempted fate with one taste of meth and had been consumed by it. Since then, he had graduated to crack and heroin.

Though it drove Jack crazy, he allowed Finn to bring the painfully thin man inside the gym after hours for a shower and a meal a few times a month. After watching Finn fight and slay his own demons, Jack would never question his younger brother's desire to help others battling addiction. He didn't think Flea could be helped—if the man survived another winter, Jack would be shocked—but Finn wasn't about to stop trying.

"Was it the money? Is that what this is about? Are you pocketing the cash from the sales of those ghost barcodes?"

"Yes."

Something about his tone told Jack there was more behind that answer. Antsy, he rubbed his thumb along the underside of his wrist and fought the urge to barge back into the storeroom to ask more pointed questions. If Abby didn't get the full truth out of Dan, he would find a way to get it on his own.

"But, Dan, if you needed money, you could have come to me. I would have given you whatever you needed, on whatever terms would have worked for you. My God—you've been a part of my family's business for decades. Granddad trusted you. He loved you like a brother—"

"Some brother," Dan interjected testily. "I gave twenty-nine years of my life to this damned shop, and where am I today? Night manager!"

"That's bull, and you know it, Dan! I offered you the general manager position, but you declined it."

"Because I'm better than that! I deserve more than a new title and a heavier keychain."

"What do you want, Dan? What is this really about?"

"I should be a partner! I ought to own part of this shop."

Jack held his breath as the tense silence stretched into long seconds.

"Dan, Granddad was always very clear that this was going to stay a family business. It was his dad's business first, then his, and now it's mine. That doesn't mean you aren't incredibly valued. If you had come to me—if you had told me how disrespected you felt by the GM offer—I would have found a way to make it work."

Jack's throat tightened as Abby's voice wavered. His sweet girl was on the verge of tears—and it killed him that he wasn't in there to support her.

"I've always thought of you as family, Dan. Even with all the friction we've had over Mattie, I always respected your position here and your knowledge of this business. Some of the best skills I have were learned from you." She paused and seemed to be trying to compose herself. "If you had asked me for a partnership in the business yesterday, I would have figured out a way to give you a slice of it—but now? Now, I want you to leave."

"You're firing me." Dan wasn't asking. He seemed resigned to the fact.

"I'm not sure. Probably," she added. "I need to sort this stolen property thing out first. I...I don't want to see you around the shop for a week. I'll make sure you get your direct deposit on the first of the month. After that...I just don't know."

Jack moved to stand in front of the door. Arms crossed, he waited for Dan to exit the room. The older man looked crushed by his dismissal, but Jack didn't feel even the slightest twinge of sympathy. He had no one to blame but himself. With a dead-eyed stare, Jack made sure Dan understood that if anything happened to Abby, he would make sure the disgraced employee was dragged through the mud.

Just thinking about the way Dan had come down like a damned hammer on Mattie for taking the watch infuriated Jack. All the while, the rat bastard had been selling stolen merchandise to unsuspecting buyers while putting Abby at great risk. It sickened him.

Sensing Dan wouldn't make a scene and didn't need to be followed, Jack returned to the storeroom.

The betrayed and wounded look on Abby's face slashed at him. He vowed then and there that he would *never* do anything to make her look at him like that. Whatever it took, he would do right by her.

He closed the distance between them. She didn't try to stop him when he reached out to wipe away the bitter tears streaking down her cheeks. The thin streams left shiny trails on her silky brown skin. He silently prayed he would never be the cause of such pain. "I'm so sorry, Abby."

"I'm stupid. You know?" She inhaled a sharp breath. "How could I not know this was happening in my store? Four weeks, Jack. The items I pulled off the shelves today date back four weeks!"

"You trusted your team, Abby. You said it yourself. Dan was a trusted member of your staff. Why would you ever suspect him of doing anything to hurt the business?"

"I should have known, Jack. I should have seen that he was upset and hurt when Granddad didn't leave him a piece of the business."

"Abby, you're not a mind reader." He used the bottom of his Connolly Fitness T-shirt to wipe away wetness still gleaming on her beautiful face. "What are you going to do?"

"I've shut down the sales side of our business. We'll continue to pawn and buy, but not one single piece of merchandise is leaving this store until I know that everything on the shelves is legit."

"And after that?"

She swallowed hard. "After that, I'll be calling my contact in the police department. I've spoken to our lawyer. It's going to be messy, and we'll have to issue refunds to all of the customers and—"

"Sweetness," he gently touched his finger to her sensual pout. "Is there anything you have to do tonight?"

"I need to finish sorting through the piles of inventory Marley helped me pull."

"Does it have to be done tonight?"

"Well—"

He seized on her moment of indecision. "We're leaving. I'll come with you in the morning and help you do whatever needs to be done."

"Jack, you have a business to run. You have clients. You have—"

He bent down and captured her lips in a searing kiss. When her protests were quieted, he pulled back just enough to gaze down into those coffee-colored irises. "You are my number one priority, Abby. The gym, my clients—none of that matters without you."

Surprise filtered across her face. "Do you...do you really mean that?"

"I said it. I mean it."

She placed her hand on his chest and stared up at him with such uncertainty. "What are we doing, Jack? What is this?"

With everything going wrong in her business, she didn't need upheaval or uncertainty in her personal life. Wanting to soothe her, he brushed his fingers along her jaw. "I'm doing what I should have done a long time ago. I'm going after the woman I want."

"Me?"

He tapped the tip of her nose. "You."

She bit her lower lip. "You're sure?"

He chuckled. "Yes, Abby. I'm sure."

"But—"

"No." He pressed his finger to her lips and repeated his earlier statement. "I said it. I mean it."

She seemed to finally understand what he was trying to tell her. Like Mattie, he was a man of his word. She needed to realize that she could always count on hearing the absolute unvarnished truth from him.

The taut stress that had been tightening her expression melted. The corners of her mouth lifted, and her eyes sparked mischievously. Like a naughty little kitten, she bit down playfully on his fingertip and touched the very tip of her pink tongue to his flesh. The brief contact ignited his desire for Abby. Suddenly, he couldn't get her home fast enough.

"Mattie is hanging out with Finn tonight, so we have your house to ourselves."

Her neatly shaped eyebrows lifted with mock annoyance. "You fix one dishwasher and one window, and now you're acting like you own the place."

Though she said it with a teasing smile, he heard the light censure in her voice. "Abby, would it be all right if we spent the night at your place? Just the two of us?" He lowered his face and dotted ticklish kisses along the curve of her neck. "You. Me. A bottle of wine. A hot bath." He bit down gently, just enough to make her inhale a shaky breath, and then flicked his tongue over the reddened spot. "What do you say, Abby?"

Shivering against him, she grasped his hand. "Take me home, Jack. Make me forget about the awful day I've had."

Her husky, needy voice spilled over him like a silky caress that went right to his throbbing dick. Before the night's end, he planned to be buried to the hilt in Abby's slick heat, but first he would give her everything she wanted. All of this bullshit with Dan would be a distant memory once he tucked her close and let her drift off to sleep in his arms, sated and relaxed.

Already forming his plan of sensual attack, he gave her hand a tug and took the lead. He would have Abby sobbing with ecstasy and screaming his name in pleasure before he was done with her.

5 CHAPTER FIVE

Eyes closed, I sank a bit deeper into the steaming hot bath. The soothing warmth eased the ache from my shoulders and neck. I tipped the glass of wine to my lips and enjoyed a long, slow drink of the slightly sweet Australian Riesling.

"You need me to top that off before I slide in with you?"

A smile played upon my lips at the deep timbre of Jack's voice. "No, thanks. I'm a one glass a night girl."

"You can let loose tonight, Abby. I'm here, and Mattie is perfectly safe with Finn."

"I'm good." Though I was tempted to have another glass, I stuck to my rule. Finally opening my eyes, I glanced at Jack and nearly had a heart attack. He had stripped down to just his boxer-briefs and—oh my God—he looked absolutely delicious. Last night, when he has slipped into bed with me, he had stayed almost totally clothed, just in case more trouble had arrived on my doorstep. Tonight, I was getting a much desired look at the full package.

And I do mean the *full* package. Already rock hard, his long, thick cock jutted out against the gray fabric of his boxer-briefs. The outline of his massive shaft told me I was going to be one very satisfied woman. Just as Jack handled everything else in life, I had no doubt that he would soon prove to be an incredible lover.

Not showing the least bit of discomfort, he confidently peeled out of his underwear and dropped them onto his small pile of clothing. He motioned for me to sit forward in the tub and climbed in behind me. Water and bubbles sloshed over the edge and spilled onto the towels he had smartly arranged beforehand. Leave it to Jack to be prepared for every eventuality.

Those big, strong hands settled on my shoulders. I melted back against him, loving the way his hot, hard body pressed to mine. Soon I hoped to have all that heat and strength on top of me and inside me. I let out a low sigh as Jack's thumb worked a knot in my shoulder. He was so much bigger than me that his hands easily manipulated my shoulders and arms, easing out the tense, painful aches and leaving me limp and relaxed.

He grabbed one of the sea sponges I kept in a basket in the corner, dipped it into the steamy, bubbly water, and dragged it along my arm. Sipping wine and being bathed and massaged by the man I had been crushing on for years was like something out of my wildest fantasies. The luxurious experience left me feeling so feminine and pampered.

"You're awfully quiet tonight, Abs."

"Just enjoying all of this," I said, dropping my head back to his chest. "It's been a long time since I've had a break."

Jack wrapped his arms around me. "We'll have to do this more often." He kissed my temple. "Maybe we should make it a standing date. You know—the last Tuesday of every month or something like that."

I noticed the way he was dropping these subtle reminders of his intent toward me, toward us. It would be so easy to believe he really wanted a long-term thing with me, but I had been burned so many times in the past. I'd had plenty of great boyfriends over the years, but none of them had been able to handle the added responsibilities that came with my family dynamic.

But Jack was different. Although I really, *really* wanted to guard my heart, I found myself falling deeper and deeper for the sexy Marine gliding that soft sponge up and down my arms and along my belly. If ever there was a man who could be all the things I needed, it was Jack Connolly.

He was the sort of take-charge, in control man I had always craved. He ran a successful business. He was good with money. He loved his family and would do anything for them. I had seen firsthand the way he had fought to drag Finn out of his alcohol-fueled downward spiral. Even now, Jack had opened his home to the father who had abused and hurt them so he could recuperate. That said a lot about his character and his loyalty.

What I wouldn't give to have a loyal, hardworking, loving man like Jack as my partner in life. It was too easy to imagine coming home to find him making dinner with Mattie's help or working in the yard or taking care of one of the household repairs that crept up every now and then. I wouldn't have to ask. He would know it needed to be done, and he would take care of it. It would be the silent, simple way he communicated his devotion and love. *I'm here. I've got this. I'll take care of you.*

Tempted by the possibilities, I traced the tattoo on his forearm. I decided to be brave. "I've had a crush on you since you walked into the shop that morning to pawn your motorcycle." Jack started to laugh. Miffed, I asked, "What?"

He noisily kissed my neck. "I nearly tripped over my own damn feet when I spotted you behind the counter. You were the prettiest thing I had ever seen. Hell, you were so distracting I screwed up the negotiation and walked out two grand lighter than I had expected."

Jack's admission sent a deliciously exciting flutter through my core. "Why didn't you say anything?"

"You were really young, Abby."

"Twenty is really young?"

"At that time in my life, it was. I had a lot of shit I was trying to sort out from leaving the Corps and trying to fix the gym and save Finn from the bottle. I wanted you. I wanted you so bad it fucking *hurt* to walk away from you, but I knew that I couldn't give you what you deserved."

"And now?" I held my breath and waited for his reply.

"Now I'm right where I need to be." He pulled me in a little tighter and pressed his lips to my cheek. "Now you're right where you need to be."

He palmed my breast and brushed his thumb across my nipple. The sensitive nub responded to his teasing touch and started to harden. I tried to push away the nagging voice that reminded me of my inadequacy in the bust department, but it was hard to ignore when I'd been beaten over the head with lingerie advertisements featuring lush, voluptuous figures since my pre-teen years.

Despite my hang-ups about my small breasts, Jack seemed to find them rather interesting. His gentle caresses grew more arousing. He pinched my nipples, not hard enough to hurt, but with enough pressure to make my clitoris pulse. My pussy throbbed now, the core of me heating up in anticipation of the lovemaking that would soon happen.

Like me, Jack was getting more worked up too. He nibbled my neck and teethed my earlobe while massaging my breasts. I could feel his hard cock pressing against my bottom. I wiggled my hips and lifted my backside, widening my thighs and welcoming the long length of him between them. When I reached down and wrapped my fingers around that big, thick shaft, he growled, the low, rumbling waves of it rolling through my chest. "Abby."

Smiling at the way I had so much power over him, I stroked him from the wide base of his erection to the ruddy tip and then back down again. His hot flesh filled my palm. When I slipped my other hand down to cup his sac, Jack swore softly and then grazed this teeth over the sensitive spot where my pulse beat so erratically in my throat.

Jack shifted slightly, and his cock rubbed against the slick feminine center of me. It would be so easy to lift up just a little and let the broad head of his cock breach my pussy. I could sink down on him, letting him stretch and fill me, and rock myself to a mind-blowing orgasm on the cock I had craved for so long.

But I didn't.

Yet.

Stroking Jack's shaft, I tightened my fingers and added a little more pressure. He responded as I expected he would, thrusting up into my hand and rocking against me. Letting my thighs fall apart, I dropped back against Jack's chest, molding my body to his, and welcomed his seeking hands. He used both of them to frame my pussy. His long fingers gently spread apart my folds while his thumbs settled on either side of my pulsing clit. He massaged up and down, stimulating that tiny pearl while licking my neck and teething my ear.

Jack cupped my breast in one massive paw but kept the other hand between my thighs. He played with my pussy like a master, his fingertips circling and tapping until I was shaking and panting. Nestling his face against my ear, he whispered, "I can't wait to get you in bed so I can replace my fingers with my tongue." He swirled them around my throbbing clit. "I'm going to suck this little berry into my mouth and lash it with my tongue until you come hard."

My face was so hot now. Breasts aching and nipples electrified, I closed my eyes and imagined all the things Jack described. I could just imagine the feel of his tongue on my sex, probing and flicking until I screamed his name.

"Are you going to let me eat this sweet pussy of yours, Abby?" He tweaked my nipple, making me gasp. "Are you going to let me wiggle my tongue here?" His finger slid down to my entrance. "So I can taste your honey?"

"Oh God." I hovered on the verge of a wickedly strong climax. No man had ever spoken like this in front of me. No man had ever said such erotic things. His words were like an aphrodisiac. I couldn't get enough.

"Come for me, Abby. Show me how much you want my tongue here." His finger tapped my clitoris, and I exploded with wild spasms of pure delight. Water sloshed around me, spilling over the edge of the tub, as I kicked and rocked to the rhythm he played.

"Jack! *Jack*!"

"That's it, sugar. You come for me." His fingers rubbed right through my orgasm until finally he stopped. I sagged against his broad chest. He curved his hand over my bare mound in a protective gesture. I enjoyed the ticklish kisses he peppered on my neck and lazily stroked his cock.

"Abby, we need to move this out of the tub."

Grinning impishly, I continued to stroke his cock. "Where to?"

He groaned and pushed against my hand. "Baby, you keep that up much longer, and I'm going to throw you down on the bath mat and take you right here."

An illicit thrill rushed through me. "Sexy as that sounds, I'm pretty fond of mattresses."

"Then you had better get that sweet little ass of yours moving," he urged.

Laughing, I climbed out of the tub and grabbed a towel. Jack joined me on the mat and made hasty work of wicking the moisture from his skin. I started to pick up the soaking wet towels on the floor but Jack popped my bottom. "Leave it."

"But—"

"No." He swung me up into his arms, turned sideways to get me through the door, and then tossed me onto the bed. Taken aback, I gasped and then succumbed to a fit of giggles when Jack hopped onto the mattress with me. He pinned me to the bed, grasping my small wrists in his big hand, and dragging them high overhead. My breath quickened at the taboo thrill of being held captive. Jack must have seen the spark of interest in my eyes because he nipped at my full lower lip. "Do you like being tied down?"

"I haven't ever tried anything like that," I admitted. Feeling a bit nervous but wanting to be honest, I confessed, "I haven't had sex in over a year, Jack." I calculated the time since my last serious boyfriend. "Actually, it's more like sixteen months."

"It's been a while for me too." He traced my lips with his tongue before sucking the tip of mine in the most delightfully naughty way. "We'll take our time and make it good."

Wanting to get the birth control discussion out of the way before things got too hot and heavy, I explained, "I have an IUD, but I've always insisted on condoms. I still get tested at my yearly exam."

"I haven't ever gone latex-free," Jack said. "Finn and I had our annual checkups earlier in the year so we could get better insurance rates. I'm in the clear."

I swallowed as I realized what he was suggesting. "Do you want to make love to me without...?"

"Do you want me to?"

Something about the prospect of feeling Jack fill me with his seed, even if it couldn't take hold, struck me as incredibly erotic. It would be a first for both of us and an experience we had shared with no other lovers. The idea of sharing something new enticed me.

"Yes."

He brushed his lips against mine and tightened his hold on my wrists. My body blossomed with goose bumps as he exerted control over me. Closing my eyes, I surrendered to him and welcomed his skills as a lover. There was so much Jack could teach me, and I wanted to start our first lesson.

Taking his time loving me, Jack kissed and nipped every inch of my body. His mouth traveled from my forehead to my toes before he flipped me onto my belly and traveled right back up again. When he had laid claim to me in that way, he tugged me onto my back again and dragged me to the edge of the bed.

Sinking down to his knees, Jack placed my feet flat on the mattress and rested his hands on my inner thighs. He gazed at my sex for a long time before separating the petals to examine the dewy center of me. "What do you like, Abby?"

I blinked with confusion. "What do you mean?"

"When man goes down on you, do you like fast strokes or slow? Lots of pressure or light?"

I stared at the ceiling and tried to find the courage to admit how little experience I had in that arena. "I've never... I mean..."

"None of your old boyfriends ever did this?"

"None of them," I confirmed.

"Selfish bastards," he growled.

Sliding a hand down to block him, I whispered, "You don't have to do it, Jack. I don't want you to feel obligated."

"Obligated?" He pushed my hand out of the way. "Sugar, if you only knew how many times I've imagined this while stroking myself."

"Really?" The idea that Jack had fantasized about me while finding pleasure made me dizzy.

"Really," he murmured and swiped his tongue through my folds. "I've been dying for a taste of this juicy cunt of yours."

My blood pressure skyrocketed, my blood rushing by my eardrums so fast and loud I couldn't hear anything but the *whoosh whoosh whoosh*. Jack fluttered his tongue around my clitoris, and I nearly died. I honestly could not draw a breath into my oxygen starved lungs. The soft but firm tip of his tongue circled that swollen pearl and flicked at it. The sensation was unlike any I ever could have imagined. It was so much better than my fingers or his.

Unable to contain myself, I cried out again and again and swiveled my hips. Jack grasped my waist and used his wide shoulders to hold me open for his oral assault. He did such incredible things to me, flicking and fluttering and suckling at my inflamed clitoris until I was a sobbing mess. Pleasure jolted me, and I came harder than ever before in my life. On and on the climax went, the waves of it slamming into me and dragging me deeper and deeper into the dark waters of utter ecstasy.

He wiped his mouth on my inner thigh and dragged me into the center of the bed. Pushing my thighs wide again, Jack grasped the base of his cock and nudged the weeping crown between my slick folds. He gathered my nectar on his ruddy skin and used the head of his penis to stimulate my overly sensitive clitoris before finally—finally!—sheathing himself inside me.

Head thrown back, I shouted his name and clutched at his arms. His thrusts started slow and easy as he let me acclimate to the length and girth of his impressive shaft. When I relaxed totally beneath him, Jack gathered my wrists again and pinned them to the pillow. The weight of him pressed me down, and I arched up onto my shoulders to meet his thrusts.

They were harder now, faster, and I urged him on with my whimpers and moans. Jack plundered my mouth, his tongue stabbing and taking while his cock pounded into me. In no time at all, I hovered on the verge of another mind-shattering orgasm. He must have seen the need twisting my expression because he changed his angle. Four good thrusts, and I fell over the edge, shouting his name and wishing the joyful bursts would never, ever end.

But, like all good things, they did. Whispering my name, Jack slammed forward, the force of his final thrust causing me to slide along the sheets, and touched his forehead to mine. We shared ragged breaths as he pumped his hot seed into me and shuddered against my body.

With an exaggerated groan, Jack fell onto his side. He grabbed the top sheet and dragged it over our rapidly cooling bodies. "You're dangerous, Abby."

Curling into him, I stared up at him in disbelief. "Me? Dangerous?"

"One taste, and I can tell I'll never be able to get enough of you."

"Is that a bad thing?"

"Hardly," he said with a grin and gathered me close. "Though I have a feeling we're both going to be very tired for the next few days."

Yawning, I snuggled tight and kissed his cheek. "Then we should probably sneak in a nap while we can…"

6 CHAPTER SIX

After a day spent with furious customers shrieking in my face and into my ear, I had never wanted to hit the gym more. While it seemed my lawyer's best efforts to smooth over the issues with the police department were working, the customers who had unknowingly purchased stolen goods were understandably angry and disappointed. I had issued refunds and given gift cards to stores where they could purchase brand new game systems, DVD players, and televisions. The added complication of a bad reputation was the last thing the shop needed after that robbery.

"Hey! I hoped to see you tonight." Bee Langston playfully bumped my hip as she pulled her long hair into a high ponytail. The tech goddess who had recently signed a jaw-dropping multi-billion dollar deal was dating Jack's youngest brother, Kelly. They were a perfectly matched couple, and after everything they had survived in the last few weeks, it was clear they had the strength to pull through anything. "I was so upset when I heard about the break-in at your shop and the brick through your window. Are you okay?"

"I'm fine. The shop is good too." I didn't tell her about the stolen property Dan had been fencing through my front doors. While I trusted that she would keep that info to herself, I couldn't trust the dozens of ears standing close. The word would get out soon enough, but I wasn't about to hasten it along. "How's the tech world going?"

"Busy," she said. Lowering her voice, she stepped closer and whispered, "I'm thinking about running away."

"What?"

She giggled. "Actually, I'm thinking about dragging Kelly with me on a long vacation. Just the two of us. Someplace quiet. Unplugged."

"You? Unplugged? Not possible!"

She laughed. "See? That's what I mean! I need to get away. I need to recharge. This is the perfect time to do it. I'm in between projects. My team is amazing. I need to go now before I get dragged into some new, huge undertaking."

"So go," I said and started working my way through the warm-up routine scrawled on the whiteboard at the front of the room. "What does Kelly say about a vacation?"

"He's surprisingly open to it." Bee stretched next to me and kept her voice conspiratorially quiet as she asked, "What about you and the oldest Connolly brother?"

A blush blazed across my face as I remembered our incredible night together. The morning had been just as hot. After some of the things Jack had done to me, I would never again think of breakfast in bed quite the same way. "We're good."

"Uh-huh," she said with a coy smile. "You know I want details, right? We should go out for a drink after class. We can swap yummy stories about our men."

Drinks? Swapping stories? I realized that it was the first time another woman had invited me out for some girl-time since college. After graduation, I had thrown myself into the business. Not long after that, Granddad had started getting sick and Mattie had run into some minor problems at school. My friends—well, the girls I thought were my friends—had slowly disappeared.

"I'd like that," I said, excited by the prospect of re-building my social life. "I can't tonight. Mattie's out with a friend of ours at a baseball game, and I have some laundry and household stuff I need to catch up on while he's out."

She wrinkled that dainty nose of hers. "You should really think about hiring a housekeeping service."

I chortled and kept stretching. "That's a bit pricey for me."

She rolled her eyes. "Oh, please. You know what's *priceless*? Having time to spend with your family and your friends. Running a small business is no joke, Abby. You're spreading yourself too thin. Hire help for home. Take off some of that burden."

Was she right? Would spending a little more money each month ease up the stress and time crunch I constantly felt?

A loud clap startled me. I glanced toward the front of the room where Jack and Finn now stood. They had entered while we were chatting and had completely bypassed us. Taken aback by the way Jack had gone out of his way to avoid me, I frowned and wondered what the hell that meant.

"All right, ladies. Let's get started." Jack began the class with his usual review of our previous meeting, a short lecture and demonstration of the new technique he was teaching. Once we had watched him perform the maneuver with Finn, Jack had us pair up and practice.

Bee and I squared off with each other. She had the worst form imaginable. I mean—it was shocking how badly coordinated the poor woman was! Normally, Jack stopped by to correct her but not tonight. He stayed near the front of the class and did everything possible to ignore us.

Finally, Finn stepped in and saved me from taking Bee's knee to the face by grasping her waist and tugging her back at the last second. "Whoa, killer! Watch it with that knee. You almost bruised one of my favorite girls."

"One of, huh?" Bee asked with a laugh. "Sounds like you have quite a long list."

"What can I say? I never forget a beautiful face." He winked and then stepped behind me. "You need to adjust your stance. You're off-balance, Abby."

"Oh!" I issued a soft gasp when Finn grasped my hips, his long fingers spanning my waist, and adjusted my positioning. His well-defined chest pressed to my back as he clasped my wrist and showed me a blocking move. The scent of him, the pleasing notes of chamomile and cedar, filled my nose.

"See?" He made sure to stay close to me—so close it was almost inappropriate—for a drawn out moment. When he finally stepped back, he flicked one of my earrings. "You shouldn't be wearing these hoops, sweetheart. It's dangerous." His amused gaze landed on Bee. "Especially when Miss Mayhem is your partner."

"Ass!" Bee playfully punched his arm, drawing an exaggerated *ow* from his mouth.

"Remind me to add a five dollar fine to your account."

"For what?" she demanded.

"Oh, it's a new policy. Mattie suggested it to me, and I ran with it this morning. If we hear you cuss, you owe the gym five bucks."

"For reals?" Bee asked, eyes narrowed.

"There's a sign at the front door. The new policy is right there in big, bright letters." Grinning, he left us to continue practicing. "Work on that block, Abby."

Bee and I continued battling each other, but I couldn't stop thinking about the way Jack was basically pretending I didn't exist. I wasn't stupid. I knew exactly what Finn had been doing. He was trying to make Jack jealous—but why?

A strange sensation crept up my spine, invaded my chest, and squeezed my heart. For all of Jack's beautiful words and sweetness toward me, he hadn't yet taken me anywhere. Since that explosive kiss in my kitchen, we had spent both nights since at my house. Sure, he had been publicly affectionate with me at my shop, but why wasn't he reciprocating here at his place of business?

Was that what this cold shoulder tonight meant? Was I going to be his secret? Was there something about dating me that made him nervous or uncomfortable? I didn't want to think it was that, but anything was possible.

Or was it something else? Was he worried that if his large female clientele learned he was off the market, they would go elsewhere? Was he ignoring me and making me feel this way because of his bottom dollar?

I didn't want to believe anything like that was true, but as the class continued, I couldn't dismiss what was right in front of me. Although Jack wasn't openly flirting with the other women, he was all smiles and laughs. I tried not to be hypersensitive about it, but I couldn't stop myself. Self-doubt welled up inside me until every single pore in my body was saturated.

Bee turned her back on me so we could practice an evasive move, one that required me to put my arms around her. Going through the motions, I fixed my gaze on Jack and the skimpily dressed nurse he was helping. With those tiny shorts and too-tight tank top, she looked like she would fit in on one of Besian's stages. She rubbed against Jack in the most suggestive way, her high, round bottom brushing against the front of his shorts, and smiled up at him with fluttering eyelashes.

The shock of what I witnessed overrode my common sense, and I lost my grip on Bee. She had been expecting more resistance from me and threw back her elbow too hard. I didn't stand a chance at blocking it. The pointy end of her bony little arm slammed right into my cheek and tossed me to the floor.

"Oh my God! Oh my God! Abby!" Bee shrieked like a panicked banshee and practically fell on top of me. "Are you okay? Are you bleeding? I'm so sorry! Shit. *Shit!*"

"Move, Bee." Jack's deep, calm voice cut through Bee's hysterics.

Blinking and wincing, I tried to sit up, but Jack's huge hands gently pressed on my shoulders. "Stay down, Abby. Let me look at you."

Anger surged through me. "Oh, *now* you want to look at me?"

He sat back on his heels, his eyes widening slightly. "There's no need for drama, Abby. Now let me see your cheek."

I smacked away his hand. "I don't need your help. I'm fine."

His jaw tightened. "Fine." He rose to his full height. "Finn, get her an ice pack and put her in the office."

For some reason, the way he so easily issued orders just pissed me off even more. I shrugged off Finn's helping hand and climbed to my feet. Though I had been dazed by Bee's unexpected blow, I was no longer dizzy. In fact, I was so irritated and upset that I didn't even feel much pain. Adrenaline and fury fueled my steps.

Bee rushed after me, following me to the women's locker room. "I'm so sorry, Abby. Let me take you to the emergency room. You probably need to have that checked out."

"I'm fine." I didn't want to tell her that my mother had hit me way harder than that as a child. Not wanting her to be wracked with guilt, I stopped packing my bag and gave her a hug. "I really am okay, Bee. It was an accident. I'll probably bruise, but it's okay."

"It's not okay." She looked like she was about to cry. "You're the second person I've hurt in this class. That's it." She slashed her hand through the air. "I'm done with this self-defense crap."

"Bee, this one was my fault. I wasn't paying attention. I was distracted."

"By that skank rubbing her ass all over Jack?" She easily guessed the cause. Knowing it had been that obvious hurt me even more. If Bee had seen the way that went down, everyone else had too. No one would ever believe that I had a thing going with Jack.

Well. That I *used* to have a thing with Jack.

"It doesn't matter. Obviously, I was wrong about us. I thought…well…it doesn't really matter what I thought." *Because he's just like all the rest of them.*

"If he does you dirty like this, he's a rotten bastard."

I smiled sadly. "Now you owe ten bucks."

She snorted softly and rubbed my arm. "I'll pay a thousand times that if meant you wouldn't get hurt."

"Too late," I murmured. "I already am."

Bee blinked rapidly, her eyes shimmering for me. God, but she was the sweetest soul I had ever met. Was her empathy heightened because she had recently gone through something similar with Kelly? Did she remember only too vividly how awful it felt to realize the man you were head-over-heels for wasn't as perfect as you had imagined?

"Let me take you home. You shouldn't drive after I nearly knocked you out."

"I'm driving to the shop to finish up the inventory audit." I made that last minute decision because I didn't think I could handle being alone in the house where Jack had made me feel so good only a short time ago. "It's a few blocks. I can handle it."

"If you're sure…"

"I'm sure."

"Okay." She gave me a quick hug. "Call me when you have a chance. We'll find a time to get together."

"Will do." Grabbing my backpack, I left the locker room and headed for the exit. The self-defense class still had twenty minutes or so left in it. Did Jack even care that I had been hit? Would he even realize I was gone?

Loud, heavy footsteps echoed in the empty gym behind me. I didn't have to turn around to know it was Jack. The prosthesis Finn wore around the gym had a different sound to it when he ran, with one step slightly lighter than the other. These were heavy, racing footfalls, and there was only one other man in the gym at this time of night.

"Where the hell are you going?"

"Home." I kept moving forward, my teary-eyed gaze obscuring my vision. "Away from you."

"What does that mean? Why?"

Aghast at his cluelessness, I spun around to face him. "Are you serious? You just treated me like I was nobody. You didn't even acknowledge my presence in there. You acted like I didn't matter. Are you embarrassed to be with me? Am I your dirty little secret?"

"What? Don't be ridiculous, Abby. I tried to help you after you got hit—"

"*After* I got hit," I repeated. "It took an elbow to the freaking face for you to even acknowledge my presence!"

"That's not—"

"You know what, Jack?" I held up my hand to stop whatever lame ass excuse he was about to lay on me. "I'm tired. I'm hurting. I'm leaving."

"No, you're not. I'm not letting you walk out of here when—"

"Excuse me?" I had had just about enough for one night. "I don't need your permission to do what I want. I'm a grown woman."

"You aren't acting like one."

Pushed over my limit, I snarled, "Fuck. You."

"Fuck me?" he repeated tightly. "Okay. Fine."

I gasped when Jack swept me up off the ground and tossed me over his shoulder like a damn caveman. My bag fell from my hand and hit the ground with a loud *thwap*. "What are you—? Put me down!" I smacked his back. "Right now, Jack."

Clamping an arm across my kicking legs, he didn't say a word. He carried me across the gym to the men's locker room, kicked the door closed and locked it behind him. Once we were locked inside, he lowered me to the ground and grabbed the bottom of his T-shirt. He jerked it up and over his head and tossed it aside.

"What are you doing?" I couldn't believe what I was seeing when he toed off his running shoes and peeled out of his socks.

"You wanted to fuck me."

"Are you—?" I blinked when Jack stripped out of his shorts and boxer-briefs. He sported a raging hard-on that pointed right at me. "You're insane! That's not what I meant, and you know it."

"Apparently, I don't know anything, Abby. I thought I was doing the right thing in class, but clearly I messed that up." He backed me up against the door and planted his hands on either side of me. Lowering his face, he peered into my eyes and kept me from running. "You are not a *nobody*. You are the most special person in the whole wide world to me, Abby Kirkwood."

I gulped. "But you—"

"I messed up. I'm sorry." His forehead touched mine. Our breaths mingled, and I didn't dare speak. I wanted to hear what he had to say. "I knew that I wouldn't be able to give the rest of the class the attention they needed if I got close to you. I can't think when you're close. I'm consumed with you, Abby." His fingertips moved along the bruise forming on my face. "It's dangerous business in there, as you now know."

My eyelids closed when Jack peppered gentle kisses to my aching cheek. Although it would be so easy to forgive him, I wasn't ready yet. "You let that dirty blonde nurse rub her ass all over you."

"I didn't *let* her do anything. I pulled away as quickly as possible, but I couldn't just drop her on her face, Abby." Concern darkened his green eyes. "How bad does your cheek hurt? Do you think we need to head out to an ER?"

"I've had worse."

His mouth settled into a grim line. "I hate that we have that in common."

"Parents who knocked us around?" He nodded. "It was a long time ago for me, Jack. I hardly even think about her anymore."

"I think about Pop beating the shit out of us every single time I see him."

"Yet he lives in your house—"

"He doesn't live there," Jack hastily corrected. "I tolerate his presence because of Finn. He's got that big, soft heart that makes it impossible for him to turn his back on the old bastard. Once Pop is healed up, he's out of the house and on his own again."

Jack brushed his lips against mine, seeking my forgiveness. "I'm sorry, Abby. I never wanted to hurt you, but I did."

The anguish in his voice was easily discernable. Now that I understood what he had been thinking, it was simple enough to see how it had gone pear-shaped.

I flicked my tongue along his lower lip and sucked it between my teeth before biting down just enough to make him hiss. When I released his lip and soothed the nip with my tongue, he issued a throaty groan. "Be up front with me next time, Jack. Tell me what you're thinking."

"I've learned my lesson, Abby. It won't happen again." Tilting his head, he studied my face. "What we have isn't a secret, sweetness. I want to climb up onto the roof right now and tell everyone that you're finally mine. But why did you jump to that conclusion? Why would you think that me giving you some space during class meant that I wanted to hide you?"

I traced the tattoo on his chest that linked together the initials of his brothers with the Marine Corps insignia. "There was this boy in high school..."

"I see," he said as my voice trailed off. "I'm not some stupid boy in high school, Abby. I wouldn't do that to you." He hesitated before asking, "Was it the race thing?"

The humiliation of that awful experience washed over me, the brutal waves of it just as painful and cold. "His parents did not approve, and he sure as hell wasn't ready to challenge them on it. I'm just glad I wised up before I did anything I would regret."

"You know our differences don't matter to me or anyone in my family. It's not an issue for us, so you can stop worrying about that right now. All right?"

Glad to have that awkward conversation out of the way, I nodded. "Okay."

He slipped his hands under my shirt and caressed my ribs. "Be honest with me, Abby. Are you dizzy?"

"I really am fine. Bee hits like a girl."

He chuckled and kissed my neck. "She knocked you flat on your perfect, perky ass."

"She got lucky."

"Uh-huh." He nuzzled the curve of my throat and grasped the bottom of my shirt.

When he started to drag it up my belly, I stopped his hand. "Jack?"

"You're the one who issued the invitation."

"That wasn't an invitation. I was telling you off."

"Sounded like an invitation to me," he murmured.

I didn't even try to stop him anymore. My resolve crumbled when his lips traveled along my neck and his hand slipped inside my sports bra. With the speed and efficiency of a determined man, Jack had me stripped naked and barefoot in record time. Grasping the backs of my thighs, he lifted me up and guided my thighs around his waist. The stiff length of him probed my folds but he didn't try to enter me yet.

Claiming my mouth, Jack sneaked a hand between our bodies and played with my clit. He swirled his fingertip over the tiny pearl hidden there, using the lightest bit of pressure to drive me wild. His tongue stabbed against mine, and he tested my entrance.

When he encountered the slick nectar gathering there, he groaned into my mouth. "You have the wettest, hottest pussy, Abby."

Jack's frank remark made my cheeks blaze, but he didn't care. He sucked the very tip of my tongue while gliding his middle finger deeper inside me. "Your choice, Abby. My fingers or my cock?"

I wrapped my fingers around his steely shaft and pressed it between my sensitive folds. "Fuck me, Jack. Show me that you want me." I kissed him hard and deep. "Only me."

Gripping my hips, he aligned our bodies and thrust up into me. Head thrown back, I moaned at the wicked invasion. Jack licked a long trail along the curve of my exposed throat and sucked hard on my skin. Goosebumps raced along my flesh, my skin prickling and buzzing as he did such naughty things to me. His teeth raked across the spot he had been tormenting, and my pussy clenched his shaft.

I wound my arms around his broad shoulders and enjoyed the feel of his muscles rippling beneath my fingertips. He displayed his incredible strength as he held me up and pounded into my slick sheath. I tried not to make too much noise—the echo in the locker room was horrendous—but there was no stopping my reaction to him. With one smoldering look, he made me come undone. There was no hesitancy or demure shyness when I was intimate with Jack. He wouldn't stand for it. I sensed he found my silence something of a dare. He wanted me screaming his name and totally out of control.

As good as Jack felt hammering into me, I couldn't make it over the edge. I stayed right there, so close to an orgasm I was shaking and panting. Proving that he was attuned to my needs, Jack slid an arm around my waist and pulled me away from the door. I clung to his shoulders as he carried me to the nearest long bench, his cock still buried deep inside me, and placed me gently on the metal surface.

Our bodies separated just long enough for him to straddle the bench. Jack slid home again, and I moaned at the incredible feeling of his shaft gliding in and out of me. He grasped my ankles and lifted them to his shoulders, tightening my passage and making it possible for him to go even deeper with every stroke.

Pressing his thumb to my lips, he silently urged me to lick at it. I did exactly what he wanted and then sighed with such pleasure when he started to rub my aching clitoris with the slicked pad of his thumb. I gripped his forearms, my nails biting into his skin, and whispered his name again and again. "Jack. *Jack.*"

"That's it, baby." Showing just how easily he could multi-task, Jack pinched my nipple with his other hand. I arched my back and whimpered at the delicious arc of discomfort that zinged right through me. My pussy throbbed now, and I rocked my hips to meet every one of his thrusts. His swirling thumb moved faster, flicking tight circles around my clit.

Toes curled and calves flexing, I chased that panicky, shuddering feeling that vibrated in my lower belly. Jack pinched my nipple, twisting the taut peak just a bit, and I exploded with sheer ecstasy. "*Ah!*"

Growling like a damned bear, Jack shifted between my thighs until his chest brushed against my breasts. He captured my mouth, muffling my cries of pleasure, and snapped his hips with incredible speed, slamming his cock into me again and again. The unending waves of my climax stole my breath. I burned with pleasure and grasped at Jack, holding on to his shoulders as he bent me in half and pounded into me. "Jack! *Yes!*"

"Abby." He groaned my name and shook in my arms. With his cheek to mine, he jerked a few times and spilled his seed. The spreading heat soothed me and made me feel so intimately connected to him. There was something comforting about the knowledge that this was something we had only ever shared with each other. It felt intensely special.

When Jack finally sat up, he dragged me with him, hefting me onto his lap with his thick shaft still fully embedded within me. He cupped my nape and took his time kissing me. Tongues dueling, we were perfectly content and relaxed. Only the knowledge that we were in the locker room at his gym spurred us to make ourselves presentable again.

Jack grabbed his soap and towels from his locker and tugged me into one of the shower stalls. He wasn't about to pass up the chance to get his hands back on my naked body, and after years of fantasizing about having Jack Connolly doing just that, I wasn't about to stop him. Consumed by his kisses and gentle petting, I leaned into him and silently hoped that all of our disagreements ended this way.

"What time does Mattie get back from the game with Detective Santos?" Jack asked as we got dressed.

"It will be late." I shimmied back into the black workout capris. "Probably close to midnight. Why?"

"I wanted to know if we needed to hurry home or not," Jack said, shrugging into his shirt. "You want to grab some dinner?"

"Dressed like this?" I motioned to my gym wear. "No, thanks."

"We could hit up a drive-thru," he offered. "I don't feel like cooking tonight, and I'm sure you don't either."

"Not particularly," I agreed and glanced around the locker room. "Shit."

"What?"

"I dropped my bag when you picked me up. I was so pissed at you that I didn't even think to go back and get it. My wallet and everything is out there."

"I'm sure Finn spotted it after he ended the class. He probably stowed it in the office."

My face flamed at the idea of seeing Finn or my classmates again. "I don't think I'll come back to class ever again."

"Why?" Jack asked with a laugh. "Because we made love in a locker room?" He pulled me close and kissed away my embarrassment. "This is my gym. We didn't inconvenience anyone. The only other man who might have needed to use the locker room is Finn—and I'd like to see him lodge a complaint."

"Still," I said, patting his chest. "We can't do this again. It's unprofessional. It could put you at risk."

"For?"

"A lawsuit? Bad press? People are crazy, Jack. If they can sue over hot coffee, they can sue over being subjected to the sounds of us going at it in here like a couple of horny teenagers."

He grunted and pecked my cheek. "Fine. But—at least you let me cross this off my bucket list."

"Oh?"

"Yep. *Locker Room Fantasy with Abby Kirkwood.*" He made a swiping motion. "Check."

"I'm almost afraid to ask what else might be on that list."

"You'll find out soon enough." Jack gave my backside a swat that left me tingling. "Put on your shoes. We'll grab your bag, shut down the gym, and get out of here."

When we stepped out of the locker room, Jack had to practically drag me along behind him. He gave my hand a squeeze and shot me a look that said he wouldn't let anyone say a word about what we had done. He bolstered my courage, but I was secretly relieved that the gym was totally empty except for Finn, who was wiping down equipment.

"Your bag is over there." The middle Connolly brother pointed to a nearby bench. "You might want to be more careful when you're carrying around expensive equipment like that, Abby."

I frowned at his comment. "My cell phone?"

Finn glanced up from his work. "No, that video camera."

"Video camera?" Confused, I walked over the bench and unzipped my bag. There, nestled in between my workout clothes and towel, was a video camera I had never before seen. "This isn't mine."

"It fell out of your bag when I picked it up." Finn spritzed another bench and began to wipe away the lemony cleanser. "I assumed it was yours."

"Maybe Mattie stuck it in there?" Jack suggested as he peered over my shoulder. "He brought me Pop's watch the other day. Maybe this belongs to some other customer he likes and wanted to help. Where do you keep your gym bag?"

"In my office."

"So he would have had easy access," Jack said. "Is there a barcode?"

I flipped the camera over and spotted one on the edge. "Here." My stomach flip-flopped. "And it's smudged."

Jack exhaled roughly. "It's another one of Dan's pieces."

"Yes. These things are like bad pennies! I can't get rid of them."

"Do I even want to know?" Finn asked as he came to stand next to Jack.

Because the word would be out soon enough, I explained, "Dan was fencing stolen property in the shop that he bought from Flea. He said he needed money."

"I'm not surprised. That kid of his has a nasty habit."

Surprised by Finn's remark, I glanced up at him. "What sort of habit?"

"Coke. The kid was with Flea a couple of weeks ago. One of those nights where I let Flea come in and get a shower and have a hot meal," he added. "I could tell right away that the kid was blitzed out of his mind on cocaine. I tried to get him to come to a meeting, but he wasn't ready. Last I heard from Flea, the kid was in some deep shit over some weight he had been moving on campus."

"Are you serious?" I couldn't believe what I was hearing. "Dan's son is dealing drugs at college?"

"He was," Finn confirmed. "The trouble isn't the legal kind,either. Flea said that the kid owed a lot of money to Lalo Contreras."

I swore softly. "He's tied in with one of those Mexican cartels, right?"

"Big time," Finn said. "So if Dan was trying to make money on the side in your shop, it was probably to clear away that debt."

"I would have given him the money. All he had to do was tell me how serious this was, and I would have given him whatever he needed." That was the part that hurt the most. Dan hadn't trusted me to help him. After all the years we had known each other, he hadn't believed in me.

"Turn it on." Jack issued his order and tapped at the camera. "Let's see what's on this."

"Why?"

"Because someone broke into your store the other night and took every single camera except for this one," Jack said. "What if this is the one they really wanted?"

I pushed the switch on the small device and shifted it so that both of the Connolly brothers could see the screen. There was only one thumbnail on the device so I clicked on it and waited for the video to load. At first, the light was so bright I couldn't make out the scene. The camera angle shifted quickly, and a man's naked chest was the only thing that could be seen.

When the man in the video moved back a little, the camera's focus automatically zeroed in and cleared up the image. A massive and ornate tattoo of an Aztec warrior had been inked on his sternum. It was the type of art I sometimes saw on the Latin street gangs around town. The other tattoos on his belly and chest told me the guy had seen a lot of prison time. A piece that looked like the Mexican sugar skulls sold around Halloween caught my eye. It was similar to the logo worn by one of the vicious outlaw motorcycle gangs that operated in the area. The same motorcycle club that Marley's stepdad served as vice president...

The man stepped to the side and disappeared from the shot. A big bed waited for him. I quickly picked up the fact that this was a sex tape. He called out to his lady in Spanish, urging her to hurry up and join him in their romp.

"Um..." I reached up to end the film, but Jack gently clasped my wrist.

"Leave it for a few more seconds."

"Perv," I groused softly.

He just snorted with amusement and kissed the top of my head. "I didn't hear you complaining in that locker room."

Now it was Finn who snorted with laughter. "No, but we all heard the enthusiasm."

I wanted to die, but Finn flicked my earring in a good-natured and teasing way. I started to understand that this was the sort of ribbing I could expect in the future. If Jack had his way, I would be hanging around with the Connolly family for a long, long time.

On camera, a scantily clad woman bounded into the shot. She was a pretty younger woman, younger than me even, with white-blonde hair and skin with a fake tan so new it was still on the orange end of the spectrum. Her choice of makeup styles screamed porn star or some other sex work with the deep, smoky eye shadow and thick, wet lips. Her eyebrows had been plucked thin and traced with a dark brow pencil.

The younger woman squealed with delight as the Aztec warrior tossed her down on the bed and climbed on top of her. She wrapped her thighs around the older man's waist as he ripped her clothing, leaving her naked and breathless.

"*Ay, papi*," she said in an exaggerated voice as he kissed his way down her body.

The Aztec warrior laughed, his voice husky and thick and the sort I would expect from a pack-a-day smoker. He started talking dirty to her in Spanish, the filthy phrases making the very tips of my ears go hot. I didn't know how much more of all this naughty foreplay I could watch with my lover and his brother only inches behind me. It felt intensely wrong and inappropriate.

But, before I could switch off the camera, I noticed the bedroom door, only barely visible in the mirror hanging next to the bed, swing silently open. Like some sort of slow motion horror film, I watched as a masked and gloved man dressed in black from head to toe crept into the room totally unnoticed by the amorous couple on the bed.

I gasped when he stretched a long, thin wire between his hands. With my brain refusing to compute what my eyes were seeing, I stared on in utter shock and horror as the assassin caught the Aztec warrior by surprise and wrapped the wire around his throat. With one quick and clean jerk, he garroted the tattooed man. Slapping and gagging and choking, the Aztec warrior fought valiantly, but the assassin was too skilled.

The terrified woman shrieked and tried to claw her way off the bed as the killer dropped her lover to the ground like a sack of rocks. The assassin snatched her ankle and dragged her to the edge of the bed. I didn't think I would ever forget the screeching sounds she made as the man put a knee in the center of her back, pushing her down against the mattress, and slipped the garroting wire around her throat. Squeezing and tugging, the killer choked the life right out of her, leaving her limp and dangling over the edge of the bed.

Stunned speechless by what we had just witnessed, the three of us watched the screen, unable to move and hardly able to breathe. The assassin left the room and returned with a heavy black bag that he placed on the bed. He began to set out the tools of his trade— tarps, jugs of bleach, paper towels, trash bags. When he retrieved a saw, I thought I would be sick. I handed over the camera to Jack, my fingers shaking and my stomach lurching. Just before I stepped away from the camera, the assassin on the screen peeled off his mask and revealed his face to us as he answered a call.

"Yes? It's done."

And then I understood what the break-in was about. This man—this killer—had missed a crucial piece of evidence. "Was it a hit?"

"Yes." Jack's voice was tight, strained. "A victim with those kinds of tattoos? A killer with that type of kit? This was professional. It was expensive."

"It's cartel business," Finn said knowingly. "That Aztec had the skull tattoo of the outlaw motorcycle crew that runs guns for Romero Valero out of Mexico. Who the hell would be ballsy enough to order a hit on one of his men? Someone very powerful. Someone incredibly motivated to keep it quiet." Finn combed his fingers through his hair. "This is *bad*, Jack. Really fucking bad."

The full reality of our dangerous situation hit me like a big rig truck. This was a world I knew virtually nothing about, and it was a world that could get me, Mattie, Finn, or Jack killed. There was only one man in the entire world that could advise me in a situation like this.

Certain Jack was going to flip his fucking lid, I mustered my courage and stated the obvious. "We need Besian's help."

7 Chapter Seven

Of all the things Jack had expected Abby to say after witnessing a brutal hit, the Albanian mob boss' name wasn't one of them.

"No." Jack shut the video screen and switched off the power. "He's not the type of man you go to for help."

"Ordinarily, I would agree with you," she said, "but this is an *extraordinary* circumstance." She pointed to the camera and then the three of them. "We've just seen a hit between rival cartels or gangs. That's out of our league, Jack. That's not our world. We need someone who knows the score." She gulped and hugged herself. "We need someone powerful to protect us."

"We could go to the police." Even as he said it, Jack knew it was a non-starter. There were certain things even the police couldn't do, and protecting them from a ruthless hit man was one of them.

"No way!" Abby's hand cut through the air. "Do you remember that awful car chase in January? When that guy who was in protective custody with the US Marshals was murdered by Romero Valero? If the Feds couldn't keep someone safe from him then, why would I trust them now? Why would I trust them to keep his enemies away from me or Mattie or you or Finn?"

Jack hated to agree with her. The murky, violent world of Houston's underbelly wasn't one that he understood. It left him feeling impotent and powerless. He had sworn that he would protect Abby and her brother, and now he didn't know where to start.

Except that he did. Everything Abby said was true. There were only two men in all of Houston who could help them now, but Jack only had connections— however tenuous—to the Albanian outfit.

The thought of going to Besian soured his gut, but he would do it for Abby and Mattie.

He turned to Finn, who seemed to be awaiting orders. "Tell Kelly to bunk with Bee tonight. Get his room ready for Mattie. I'll take Abby to her place to pack whatever they'll need. We'll call Eric and get him to drop Mattie at our house."

"What do I tell Kelly?"

"Nothing." Jack hated the thought of dragging his brother or Bee into this mess. "You've already seen the video, so it can't be helped." He placed his hand on Finn's shoulder and gave it a squeeze as guilt gripped him. "I'm sorry, bro."

"For what?" Finn shrugged nonchalantly. "Whether I saw the video or not, I would have gotten involved in this. Abby and Mattie mean the world to you. That makes them family as far as I'm concerned. We protect our family."

"Yes, we do." He caught Abby's panicked gaze and noticed the way she seemed to relax a little at the realization that she had the full might of the Connolly brothers behind her. Even if they tried to keep Kelly out of the loop, he would find a way to get the full story eventually. Then he would be right there with Finn, standing to shoulder-to-shoulder with Jack to fight off whoever dared to threaten one of their women.

Their plan made, Jack grasped Abby's hand and interlaced their fingers. He maintained contact with her in hopes of reassuring the woman he loved that she was going to be all right. He had no doubts that the next few days were going to be tense and dangerous, but they would find a way out of this alive and whole. There was simply no other choice for him. He had made his promise to her and he wasn't about to break it.

After Abby gathered the things she needed from her car, they locked it and left it in the parking lot. While he drove away from the gym, she traded texts with Eric. "He wants to know why I'm changing plans. What do I tell him?"

Jack considered the options. "Tell him that I screwed up the dishwasher repair and flooded the house. You're staying with us until I get the floors fixed."

Abby's thumb danced across her cell phone screen. She slipped her phone back into her bag and sat back. Her gaze drifted to the window, and he reached for her hand. He hated to interrogate her now, especially after the shock of that awful video, but it had to be done.

"Tell me about your relationship with Besian."

Her gaze snapped toward him. "Why?"

"Because I'm about to walk into the lion's den, Abby, and I need to know all the angles. I need to know the history you have with this man." The memory of his family's run-in with the gangster and loan shark twisted his gut. "Between Besian and Hagen, we nearly lost the gym and Kelly a few weeks ago. We were in deep—hundreds of thousands of dollars—and it was

Kelly's fists and Bee's selfless love for him that saved us."

Abby's sharp gasp at the mention of the dollar amounts involved convinced him she hadn't known the full extent of his family's entanglement. "My God, Jack! That's terrible. I had no idea. I mean—I had heard that your dad was on the line for some big loans, but no one ever let it slip that it was *that* much."

"I don't like Besian, and I don't like John Hagen." He wanted that clear right up front. "I think they're both scum."

"But?"

"But if keeping you and Mattie safe means I have to get down and dirty with a criminal asshole like Besian Beciraj, I'll do it."

"Jack, I would never ask you to do that." She squeezed his hand. "You're too good a man for that kind of thing. Whatever Besian wants, I'll give it to him if it means we'll all come out of this alive."

"Like hell!" He disabused her of that notion quickly. "Do you know what he does? What sort of ways he makes his money?" Jack swallowed hard at the idea of Besian calling in a favor and forcing Abby onto one of his glittered stages. "The man is little more than a pimp with his strip clubs. The chop shops he's rumored to run aren't any better. I won't even touch the lending side of his business or the gambling. No." His voice cracked like a gunshot in the truck's cab. "You aren't making any deals with him."

"I've already made deals with him, Jack."

He damned near jerked the wheel and only barely managed to stay inside his lane. "*What?*" His gaze jumped from the windshield to her face and back again. There were too many shadows for him to see her clearly. "Abby, what kind of deals?"

"When Granddad was alive, he had a long-running deal with Afrim Barisha, Besian's old boss. He would send his clients to our shop to make payments when they didn't have cash. They brought in merchandise to be pawned and took their cash to the loan shark. Granddad sold the merchandise to recoup the loaned money they weren't going to repay and Afrim would settle up with a five percent kickback."

"Jesus, Abby!" He couldn't believe Mr. K had done such crooked dealings. "Does anyone else know?"

"No."

"Not even Dan?"

"No, not even Dan. If he had, don't you think he would have used that information to force me to give him money for whatever trouble his son is in or to force my hand on a partnership percentage?"

She had a point.

"Well. Actually, I guess Eric knows. He thought the attempted break-in a few weeks ago and this new one might have been connected. He worried it was tied to Besian. Like, maybe he was trying to intimidate me."

"Is he?" Jack wouldn't put it past the bastard.

"No. We have an understanding."

Remembering the warning Detective Santos had given him, Jack decided he wanted the truth. "Are you still taking payments?"

"No. It stopped the day I realized what had been going on, right around the time Granddad had that last heart attack and Besian's boss was stuffed in that trunk. We had a sit-down and agreed the partnership had only existed between those two men so we would have to negotiate a new deal to move forward. I didn't want a new deal, and Besian let me walk."

"Just like that?" Jack didn't believe it for a second.

She hesitated. "I promised him that I wouldn't allow any other crews to operate out of my store and that I wouldn't pay protection money to anyone else."

"Do you pay him a protection tax now?"

"No, but he took care of that thing with the brick."

Jack couldn't believe what he was hearing. The thought of Abby going to a fucking mobster behind his back slashed at him. "Did you go to him for help?"

"No, he came to me. He visited the shop yesterday to tell me that he had taken care of it. The 1-8-7 crew won't bother me again."

"And what did he want in return for this favor?"

"Nothing."

"Bullshit. Besian Beciraj doesn't do nice things for anyone without expecting something in return."

"He didn't ask me for anything, Jack. Honestly, I think this was more about strengthening his position than anything. Now that John Hagen has left the sharking business, it's up to Besian to capture the market share from Hagen's successor. Besian's outfit has been growing, and their territory is expanding. It makes sense that he would want the 1-8-7 gang off my block. It's a bigger buffer for him and his interests."

"I don't like it."

"Neither do I, Jack, but we're in a precarious position here." She picked up the camera and placed it on her lap. "If Finn is right and the guy killed in this video was tied in with Romero Valero, that's really bad. His reputation is terrifying. Like—I've heard he carries a machete!"

Jack had heard the stories too. Kelly was friends with Vivian, Romero's daughter who had married mob boss Nikolai Kalasnikov. That was a tangled mess of a family tree if he'd ever seen one! But Kelly had told him the rumors of her father, and they weren't very encouraging. If that video was evidence of one of his men being killed, Romero would want it, and he would do anything to get his hands on it.

Then there was the hit man who had made the mistake of showing his face on the video. There were two possibilities there. One, Flea had realized after fencing the stolen goods to Dan what he had given away, so he had broken into the shop hoping to get it back and save himself. Two, drug-addled Flea had run his mouth to the wrong person and now the word was on the street about the video. Jack leaned toward scenario number two because Flea wasn't smooth enough to break into Abby's shop, steal the electronics, and get out without leaving evidence.

But who was smooth enough? The assassin? Sure. One of Romero Valero's men? Definitely. The person who had hired the assassin? Absolutely.

The tightness in Jack's chest spread as he realized how many people could be looking for that video camera. All of them would easily put a bullet in Abby or Mattie to get it back. For the assassin, especially, it was important to silence the few people who had seen his face.

Considering the trouble they were about to bring to Besian's front door, Jack questioned whether the man would even be willing to help them at all. He didn't need the added heat of a cartel and a gun-running ex-felon with an outlaw motorcycle gang on his payroll. It could get messy very fast.

When they pulled into the parking lot of the high-end strip club that the Albanian owned, Jack heard Abby giggle and glanced at her with confusion. "What's so funny?"

"This is the first place you've ever taken me," she said, unlatching her seatbelt. "Our first public foray, and we're headed to a strip club."

Jack cringed. He hated the idea of taking Abby into the place, but he wasn't about to leave her outside in the truck. "When this all blows over, I swear I'll take you out on the town, Abby. I'll wear a suit. We'll go to a nice restaurant. I'll rent a suite in a downtown hotel. Flowers, wine, chocolate—whatever you want."

"Does that include jewelry?" she asked with a playful smile.

Smiling, he leaned over to kiss her. "I happen to know a girl who can get me a forty percent discount on some really nice diamonds."

Abby's mouth curved with amusement. "Forty percent? Don't push your luck."

Glad to have this moment of levity in their stressful situation, Jack laughed and pressed his lips to hers. She slid her hand along his arm and up to the back of his head. He stabbed his tongue into her mouth, tasting her, and made sure to push all the passion and love he held for her into their kiss. He bit down gently on her lower lip, plumping it up with the nip of his teeth, and marking her just enough for her to remember that she was his.

Caressing his cheek, she said, "Let me do the talking at first. Besian likes me. He'll help me."

Jack nodded stiffly. "If that's what you want."

"I trust that you'll know when to step in," she added before pecking his cheek. "You have good instincts."

Praying those instincts would guide them out of this successfully, he slid out of the truck and walked around to Abby's door. He used those old skills to scope out the area, taking note of the vehicles surrounding theirs in the parking lot and the traffic on the street. Not for the first time, he wished he had one of his pistols on him. The one Finn had packed for him was locked away in Abby's closet. God help them if someone decided to open fire.

When they made it to the front entrance of the club, the bouncers barred them from entering. A sour-faced man shorter than Jack by half a foot shook his head. "We have a dress code."

Smiling sweetly, Abby stepped forward. "Can you please tell Mr. Beciraj that Abby Kirkwood is here? I'm sure he'll make an exception. It's a business issue."

The bouncer studied her for a moment. "Wait here."

Jack grasped Abby's elbow and gently guided her into a well-protected spot, using the building and cars to shield her from anyone who might be following them. He slid into a guarding position that covered her exposed side, using his own body to block any bullets that might come flying their way. He didn't think anyone would be dumb enough to open fire at the front door of the Albanian mafia, but the people potentially after the video camera tucked into Abby's backpack were probably desperate enough to try.

When the short bouncer returned, he flicked his fingers. "Mr. Beciraj will see you. Follow me."

With his hand between her shoulder blades, Jack followed Abby into the club. He could tell by her wide eyes that she had never been in a place like this. When she glanced at him and frowned, he sensed she could tell that he had. It wasn't his scene anymore, but as a young Marine between tours, he had frequented such joints. Well—not places as nice as this one. Whatever his feelings toward the mobster, Jack had to admit the club was lavish and upscale and every bit the gentleman's club it claimed to be.

They were led across the bustling main floor to a door hidden by purple crushed velvet drapes. The short bouncer took them down a hall lined with doors, most of them dressing rooms and employee lounge spaces to a suite of offices at the rear. He motioned toward a door and left them.

Abby rapped her knuckles against the door, and Jack instantly took note of the solid sound it created. Clearly Besian expected trouble if he had a door like that one separating him from the rest of the club.

"Yes?"

Almost timid now, Abby pushed the door open and peeked inside. "Besian?"

"Abby! Come in!" The mobster's warm greeting was quite unlike the reception Jack and his brothers were used to receiving. Though it twisted his gut to seek help from a man so mired in the seedy underworld of Houston, Jack was nonetheless encouraged by the mobster's apparent happiness at seeing Abby.

Following close on her heels, Jack swept his practiced gaze around the interior of the office. He immediately noticed the second man leaning against the wall behind Besian's desk. He recognized the man with that ice cold gaze as Kostya, one of the associates of Nikolai Kalasnikov. The Russian had helped Kelly a few weeks back when his youngest brother had been looking for the jackass extorting Bee over those graphic photos of her brother.

Bolting out of his chair, Besian rushed around the desk. "What the hell happened to your face?" The mobster glared at him. "Did he hit you?"

Jack put a hand on Besian's chest, stopping the man before he could touch her. "I've never hit a woman in my life. Can you say the same?"

Besian's eyes narrowed. "Bruising the merchandise wouldn't be good for business."

The cold answer fit Jack's estimation of the man. Before the situation could get even tenser, Abby explained her slightly swollen cheek. "A girl in the self-defense class whacked me with her elbow."

Never one to pass up the chance to insult him, Besian remarked, "It sounds as if you need a better teacher."

"Besian," Abby said in a slightly pleading tone. "Please. Can we not do this tonight?"

"Fine." The strip club owner returned to his chair and leaned back, sliding both hands behind his head. "So, Jack, how are you?"

Jack leveled a chilly stare at the mobster. "Peachy. You?"

Besian laughed. "Business is fantastic. I can't complain."

"Happy for you."

Clearly wanting to head off a confrontation, Abby stepped in front of him. She gripped her backpack tightly in both hands. Though Jack couldn't see her sweet face, he easily read the concern that immediately darkened Besian's expression. The bulldogging was forgotten, and he dropped his hands to the desk. "Abby, why are you here?"

"I need your help." Her voice cracked, and Jack could only imagine how hard it was for her to come in here and ask for the mobster's protection. Not that it was any easier for him...

"Did those little punks come back? I swear to God—I'll put every last one of them into the hospital if—"

"It's not the 1-8-7 crew. It's this." She placed her backpack on his desk and unzipped it. With shaking hands, she removed the camera and passed it over. "I think this was what the person who broke into my shop wanted."

Besian's dark eyebrows arched as he accepted the camera from her. "I don't understand."

"There's a video on it. Only one video," she added. "And it's gruesome."

"Gruesome?" The Russian interjected himself in the conversation. "Death?"

Abby's head bobbed. "A murder."

Turning on the camera, Besian found the video and hit play. With the Russian glancing over his shoulder, the Albanian mafia boss watched the brutal hit without even the slightest bit of shock or horror showing on his face. His emotionless coal-black eyes didn't flicker away from the screen for even an instant.

In that moment, Jack realized Besian Beciraj was even more dangerous than he had ever thought. Any man who could watch that violent slaying without displaying any feelings of remorse or disgust was a man capable of unspeakable acts. One quick look at Kostya, and Jack understood that these two men had earned their reputations through ruthless viciousness. The Russian seemed to be critiquing the crime playing out in front of him, his judgmental expression at times approving, and at others disapproving.

When the sound of crinkling plastic filled the air, Besian shut the screen and glanced at his Russian counterpart. An unspoken discussion occurred between the two men, one that Jack simply couldn't decipher. Unsettled, he went rigid and tried to read their body language. Had this been a massive mistake? Were they in even more danger now?

Finally, Besian looked at Abby. "Who else has seen this?"

"Just me and Jack."

Keeping his face a mask, Jack didn't let on that she had lied. While he thought it might be a bad move, he understood her desire to protect Finn from the fallout of the camera's discovery.

"The girl in this video worked at one of our strip clubs. At Sugar's," Besian said. "Tawny has been missing for two weeks. We thought she had run off with her old man." He tapped the video camera. "This guy. His name is—*was*—Mando Fernandez. He was the sergeant-at-arms for the Calaveras motorcycle crew that runs protection and guns for Romero Valero. He's probably the closest thing Romero had to a best friend."

Jesus. It was just as bad as they had thought. "The hitman? He's from a rival gang? A cartel?"

Besian held his gaze. "He's freelance and a former spec ops guy. Fuck. You probably worked with him when you were playing soldier over there."

Jack let the dig slide. "Delta? Rangers? SEAL?"

The mobster shrugged. "I couldn't tell you. He's a myth. Fantazmë. A ghost," he translated from his mother tongue. "You contact him through a handler. You make the payment. He makes the hit. End of story."

"Except now we know what he looks like." Kostya said what they were all thinking. "That's not good for business."

"No," Besian agreed quietly.

"Please, Besian," Abby whispered pleadingly. "Tell me what to do."

"Nothing." Besian handed over the video camcorder to the Russian. "This isn't something a nice girl like you handles. I'll take care of this. You stick close to

Jack. If there's one thing these Connolly men do well, it's protect their own."

Jack locked eyes with the mobster. Whatever animosity existed between them, it was clear that Besian would set that aside to ensure Abby's safety. For some reason, Besian felt intensely protective toward her. Jack doubted he would ever respect the gangster, but he could stomach working with him on this.

"Abby, step outside for a minute. I need to speak to Jack alone."

She glanced back at him, unsure whether to follow the order or not. Jack didn't like the idea of being separated from her. The Russian stepped forward. "I'll guard her. She'll be safe with me."

Jack decided the devil he knew was better than sending her out into the hall alone where anyone could get at her. He nodded at Abby, who reluctantly gathered up her backpack and left with Kostya close behind her. Alone with Besian, he waited for the other man to speak.

"There's no love lost between us, Jack, but I need you to understand that is all in the past for me. Abby's grandfather was a good partner with my predecessor, and she lives in my territory. Whatever you might think of me, I believe in loyalty above all things."

"Even money?" Jack couldn't help himself.

Besian cracked a smile. "Even money."

Gesturing to the camera Kostya had put on the corner of the desk, Jack asked, "How bad is this? And don't bullshit me, Besian."

"It's bad. Ever since Romero Valero killed that witness against his old cartel, he's been making moves south of the border and building up his business. There's friction between Romero and Lorenzo Guzman."

"The drug lord?"

"Yes. We've tried to keep Houston quiet—"

"We?"

"My associates and I," Besian said, refusing to name names. "We've managed to keep a lid on the problems here, but that?" He pointed to the camera. "That could set off a fucking war. It might be personal, but only the council can green light a kill between rivals within the city. If that wasn't a personal issue, it was a cartel sanctioned hit that broke the rules, and that's a problem for all of us."

Sucking in a noisy breath, Besian rose from his chair and scratched his fingers through his black hair. "The only man who can give Abby full coverage on this video is out of town. Kostya will tell me if he can provide some backup on this until I'm able to speak to his boss. If he agrees to help, it won't be cheap."

And there it was. The moment he had been expecting.

Jaw clenching, he asked, "What do you want?"

Besian issued a sharp laugh. "The better question is what are you willing to give me?"

"For Abby? Anything."

"Even your gym? Your house?" The mobster held his gaze. "Your life?"

He didn't hesitate to give his answer. "Take them."

Besian studied him for an unnervingly long moment. "No, I think I'll take something else."

Jack didn't like the sound of it but he couldn't be picky. He needed this man's help. "And what is that?"

"Your integrity."

Gut twisting, Jack slashed his hand through the air between them. "If you think I'm going to go out and hurt someone for you—"

"That's not what I had in mind," Besian interrupted. "I have men who take care of that already. No, what I need is a driver."

Jack's eyes narrowed. "A driver?"

"Yes."

"For?"

"You'll find out tomorrow night. Do you know Merkurie Motors and Towing?"

It was the automotive shop and towing company that Besian owned. "I know where it is."

"Be there by seven tomorrow evening." The mobster picked up a business card and scribbled a number on the back. "You can reach me here at any time. It's my personal number."

Feeling as if he had fallen down the rabbit hole, Jack took the business card. He grabbed the camera from the corner of the desk. Besian started to stop him but Jack shook his head. "Abby needs this as a bargaining chip. It stays with her. I'm not about to let her become some fucking pawn that you criminal pricks use to one-up each other."

"Careful, Jack," the Albanian warned. "This criminal prick is all that stands between you and the same wire that choked the life out of those two people." Dismissing him, Besian opened the door of his office. "Be safe tonight, Jack. I'll send my men to sit on Abby's house."

"She and Mattie are staying with me."

"Then I'll send them to your house."

Jack's skin crawled at the thought of mob enforcers sitting on his house, but he grudgingly acknowledged it was the safest thing for Mattie and Abby. He wanted to choke on his tongue, but he uttered a quick, "Thank you," before whisking Abby out of the strip club and into his truck.

They didn't speak on the drive to her house. He had a feeling she was too terrified or feeling too guilty to ask what he had promised Besian during their chat. Hating that he compromised himself by agreeing to meet Besian at the auto shop, Jack acknowledged there was no other way. The decision was simple enough. Abby's life or his integrity? Abby won hands-down every time and without question.

When they reached her home, he parked in the driveway and walked around to collect her from the passenger side. Shielding her, he put Abby between his body and the house. Jack constantly scanned their surroundings. Once they were inside the house, he relaxed a little but not much. "Be quick about it, Abs. Just grab what you and Mattie need for tonight. We'll come back in the morning to get whatever else you'll need."

She looked as if she wanted to ask him a million questions, but she held her tongue and rushed off down the hall. He had barely turned back to glance out the newly replaced window when he heard her panicked voice calling to him.

"Jack! Hurry!"

Heart in his throat, Jack rushed to find her. Frozen like a statue, Abby stood next to her bed. The bedside lamp illuminated her room, and it wasn't until he stepped up behind her that Jack spotted the items left on her bed.

A long, menacing garroting wire. A picture of Mattie. A slip of paper with a phone number.

Hauling Abby tight to his chest, he wrapped her in his arms and kissed the top of her head. Her terrified tears soaked the front of his shirt. Soothingly rubbing her back, Jack felt that icy resolve that had gotten him through his tours of duty seeping from his core and spreading into his chest.

This assassin had just made the biggest fucking mistake of his life.

CHAPTER EIGHT

Curled up in Jack's bed later that night, I anxiously awaited his return. Ever the protector, he was going through the house, checking windows and doors. I could only imagine the immense amount of stress he felt right now. Taking on the responsibility of keeping us safe must have been a tremendous weight for Jack to bear, but surprisingly, he seemed calm and cool about the whole thing.

I had noticed an immediate change in him since finding that stupid video camera in my bag. It was as if someone had flipped a switch inside Jack. He was no longer the civilian I had come to love so much. He was a hardened Marine, ready to strike at any moment. Going to Besian for advice and help had been difficult for him. I had seen the tightness in his jaw and the clench of his fingers, and I loved him all the more for being practical enough to admit when he was out of his depth.

We had never navigated the murky waters of Houston's criminal element. We didn't know the score between all these crews. We didn't know about the long history of bad blood between the outlaw motorcycle gang and the cartel. We sure as hell had no idea about hiring a hitman—or calling him off.

My gaze fell on the slip of paper sitting on the bedside table. I hadn't yet called the number. What was I going to say? "Oh, hey, about that video camera someone fenced in my store...? I showed it to a mob boss you might know..."

Yeah. *That* was going to go over really well.

Jack had called Besian on the drive back to his house to let him know the assassin had paid me a visit. To say Besian hadn't been pleased was quite an understatement. I had never in my life been happier to have friends in such unique and low places.

Because this wasn't just about me anymore. This was about Besian enforcing the boundaries of his territory and showing the full force of his ability to protect and defend those he claimed as his. He would do anything to save face and uphold his reputation around Houston.

And that meant Jack wouldn't have to put his life on the line for me. I couldn't bear the thought of the man I had loved so long being badly hurt—or worse— trying to guard me from this mess that had fallen into my lap. A warrior to the core, Jack wouldn't hesitate to take a bullet for me. I would do anything to make sure that didn't happen.

The door swung open and Jack stepped inside the bedroom. His taut expression relaxed as he swept his gaze over me and shut the door. "You look good there."

I smiled at him. "It feels good to be in your bed."

"We'll have to see about keeping you there." Jack shot me a look that promised so much. "Did you talk to Mattie?"

"Yes."

"What did he say?"

"He told me that he saw Flea selling the camcorder to Dan one evening when I was working late in the front of the shop. He was hanging out in the storeroom doing that make-believe archaeologist thing he does when he heard Dan open the back door and let Flea inside. He didn't think that it was okay for Dan to buy things that way so he waited and swiped it off the shelf."

"And stuck it in your backpack?"

I nodded. "Apparently he planned to tell me about it, but he got distracted and forgot. You know how he is about things like that."

"Yes."

"He didn't look at the video. In fact, he was really pissed at me for even suggesting he would do something so rude. I've always been able to tell when he's lying. He's telling the truth on this one. He hasn't seen the video."

Jack let loose a relieved sigh. "Well, thank God for that. It's the last complication we need."

"I agree." Though Jack and I could keep secrets, Mattie had never been able to handle them.

Jack crossed the room to sit on the end of his bed. With his broad shoulders toward me, Jack leaned down and unlaced his sneakers before peeling out of his shirt and tossing it aside. He rested his elbows on his knees and placed his head in his hands. Not for the first time, I counted all the scars marring his skin. God, what pain this man had known.

Overtaken by the urge to touch him, I pushed away the sheet and crawled toward him. I caressed his back with long, slow swipes of my hand and massaged his shoulders. I dotted kisses all along his neck and upper back. "I'm sorry about everything, Jack.

"Hush." He reached back and covered my hand with his. "You'll be safe here, Abby. We have a security system. Finn is taking the first watch downstairs. No one will touch you or Mattie."

"What happens when we have to leave your house? I have to go to work. Mattie is already talking about his art class tomorrow night." Guilt swamped me as I remembered how easily I had lied to Mattie about why we were staying at the Connolly house. Thankfully Eric had bought the lame excuse I had given. Mattie had been so excited by the prospect of kicking it in Kelly's room that he hadn't even asked any questions.

"We'll figure it out," Jack promised. "Between me and Finn and the help Besian has offered, we'll keep an eye on you two."

"And you? Who keeps an eye on you, Jack?"

"I'm a big boy, Abby." He signaled an end to that line of questioning by pushing up off the bed and turning toward me. Hands on either side of my thighs, he leaned into me, capturing my mouth in a sensual kiss that blasted away the anxiety gripping me. His tongue flicked against the seam of my lips, coaxing me to let him inside. Powerless to fight this man, I whimpered softly and granted him access. Jack's tongue dueled with mine, twirling and stabbing until I was clinging to his shoulders and throbbing all over.

He pressed me down to the bed and shoved my camisole out of the way, baring my belly and breasts to his tormenting mouth. When he sucked my nipple, I arched up off the bed, my back bowing and toes curling into the mattress. It was all I could do to stifle my pleasured cry. I clapped a hand to my mouth to muffle the sounds as Jack did wild things to my breasts, licking and suckling and nibbling at them until they ached.

He bit the waistband of my tiny boy shorts and started to drag them down my hips, nuzzling his nose against my mound as he revealed my naked pussy. Keenly aware that my brother was cross the hall and his was downstairs with his father, I protested his determined onslaught. "Jack," I whispered in a begging tone. "We can't. Finn, your dad, and Mattie—"

"Hush," he gently admonished and whisked away my undies. "I can be quiet. Can you?"

He rubbed his mouth side to side against the plump lips of my sex. My clit pulsed with anticipation. "You know I can't. Not when you're doing such wicked things to me."

He peppered noisy kisses up and down the seam of my pussy. "If you want it bad enough, you'll find a way."

The daring way he said it warned me I was in for the tongue-lashing of a lifetime. Grasping my thighs,

Jack spread them wide open and swiped the pointed tip of his tongue between my folds. He zeroed in on my clitoris, fluttering over the little pearl, and then suckled it with long, slow tugs. Unable to help myself, I lifted up on my elbows and watched the drop dead sexy Marine with his face buried between my thighs. The sight of strong, powerful Jack kneeling at the edge of the bed to pleasure me did crazy things to my heart.

Falling back to the mattress, I sifted my fingers through his dark hair and concentrated on the delicious sensations that skilled tongue of his evoked. He had quickly learned the combination to unlock all the frenzied passion within me. The right pressure, the right speed—Jack gave me exactly what I needed.

My toes bit into the mattress, and my thighs flexed as I swiveled my hips just a bit. He slid his hands under my bottom, cupping my flesh in both hands, and delved into my pussy with wild abandon. I covered my mouth with my hand and tried to maintain enough control not to shriek as Jack's tongue wiggled side to side across my clit. Any second now...

"*Uh!*" Breathing hard and desperately trying to contain the ear-piercing shriek that threatened to erupt from my throat, I undulated atop the bed, hips jerking and fingers clawing at the quilt beneath me. Wicked, wicked Jack just kept right on pushing me, his tongue fluttering and flicking until he sucked my swollen bud between his lips and sent me reeling head first into another even more shockingly wonderful climax.

Shuddering and panting, I hadn't even managed to open my eyes when he roughly flipped me onto my belly and grasped my hips. He hauled me up onto my knees, pressed his cock between the slick petals of my pussy and thrust deep. I bit my lip and pushed back against him, desperate to feel him taking me long and hard.

With all the danger that surrounded us, I needed this connection to Jack more than anything. The way he pumped into me, his fat dick pounding into me again and again, told me Jack craved the same thing. When he gripped my hair in a tight fist, I nearly exploded again. An illicit thrill rocked me, my pussy clenching his shaft as it glided in and out of my slick heat. He had never been rough with me, but the small taste had me wanting more.

Jack must have realized that I liked it because he pulled a little harder, urging me into a kneeling position. With one hand clutching my hair, he used the other to squeeze my breasts and pinch my nipples. I had never felt anything like this. The changed angle in his penetration made me see stars. He stroked deep inside me, bumping up against the entrance of my womb and rubbing that sensitive spot that made my damned thighs quiver.

Lips against my ear, Jack whispered harshly all the dirty things he planned to do to me when he took me to that hotel suite he had promised me. I imagined all the erotic delights in store. Jack never broke a promise. Soon enough, I would know what it felt like to be tied up, spanked, and fucked with total abandon, to be left weeping and trembling with pleasure overload.

"Touch your clit, sweet baby." Jack bit my earlobe and then nibbled the curve of my neck. "I want to feel this wet cunt milking my cum."

This uber-alpha, dominating side of Jack made my head spin. I gulped in air and slid my hand down my belly to the juncture of my thighs. His cock glided in and out of me, his strokes faster now and his erection steely and thick. Stretched and filled by the man who had owned my heart since the first time he had flashed a smile my way, I strummed my inflamed clit. One sharp tweak of my nipple and Jack shoved me over the edge.

His hand clamped over my mouth, muffling the noisy moan that escaped my lips. He sucked hard on my neck, marking me as his with his lips and teeth, and slammed so deep inside me that my knees came up off the mattress. Suspended in his powerful arms and balanced on his cock, I shook like a leaf and rode wave after incredible wave of blissful ecstasy.

We collapsed to the bed in a sweaty, shuddering heap of tangled limbs. Jack curled up to my back, tucking his knees beneath my bottom, and caressed my bare skin. His callused palm followed the outline of my belly and breasts before touching my cheek. He turned my face ever so gently and claimed me with a tender kiss.

Grinning teasingly, he said, "We're pretty good at this quiet sex thing."

I giggled. "I don't know about that. Mattie will sleep through a tornado, but Finn?"

"He's a grown man. If he heard anything, he won't say a word." Jack moved away just long enough to peel off his socks and step into a pair of shorts. He tossed my panties back at me. "Put those on. Where are your shoes?"

"Over there," I pointed to the chair in the corner.

He retrieved the shoes and dropped them on my side of the bed. "Just in case," he said before leaning down to switch off the lamp.

"Just in case...?"

"Just in case we have to run." He opened the drawer on his side of the bed and removed a mean looking pistol. An expert with weapons, he checked the immaculately clean handgun and set out not one but three loaded magazines.

Though I was a firm believer in the Second Amendment and had made a tidy sum on firearm sales, I was also understandably nervous about having weapons out in the open. "Jack, please be careful with that. Mattie has always followed the safety rules Granddad put into place, but he's so curious about things."

"I'll lock it up in the morning." He turned off the lamp on his side and slid into bed with me. "Finn and I have already checked the gun safe in the den. We've got two weapons out, one for him and one for me. Both are in our hands or at arm's reach at all times. Mattie won't get close to them."

"I'm not trying to be a nag."

Jack hauled me against his body and pressed my cheek to his chest. "You're a good sister. I understand why you're worried. Mattie is lucky to have you." He kissed my forehead. "You're going to be an amazing mother."

"I don't know about that."

"I do." He spoke firmly and brushed a damp curl from my face. "You're loving and patient. That's all it takes."

Drawing my initials on his chest, I admitted, "Sometimes I worry that I'll be like my mom."

His arms tightened around me. "I worry that I'll be like my dad."

"You won't." I believed that with every fiber of my being.

His lips brushed my forehead again. Rather pensively, he asked, "Do you want kids?"

"Sure."

"Soon?"

My heart skipped a beat. "Well...not nine months from now soon."

He laughed softly and trailed his fingertips down my arm. "I didn't mean that soon. I meant two or three years."

I swallowed hard. Was he asking me what I thought he was asking me? "That depends."

"On?" When I didn't find the courage to answer, Jack rolled me onto my back and framed my body with his larger, hotter one. His thumb grazed the apple of my cheek. "Does it depend on me?"

"Yes." I had never been more thankful for the shadows hiding my nervous expression.

Jack's thumb traced my lower lip now. "And what if I told you that I had been in love with you since the first time I saw you swinging with Mattie at the park behind the gym?"

I blinked. "What?"

His thumb slid along the cupid's bow of my upper lip. "It was a couple of weeks after I came in to get that loan from your granddad. I had taken the small class I was training to run on the trail there. You and Mattie were laughing so hard and swinging like a couple of kindergartners. It made me smile. It made me feel happy to watch you two." He went silent. "It had been a long time since I had felt that way, and for the rest of that week, I kept thinking about you, about your smile and your sweetness, and I just..." His voice trailed off to nothing. "I knew, Abby."

Feeling lightheaded, I asked, "You knew what, Jack?"

"That it was you. That it was always going to be you." He swallowed noisily. "This is all moving fast. For me, it seems like a lifetime because I've been waiting for my chance to come clean with you about how I feel, but for you—"

"I love you, Jack." I blurted out the four words in the most unromantic way possible. I didn't think he would mind though.

"Yeah?" I could hear the smile in his voice.

"Yes."

"God, I love you, Abby."

Our lips touched finally, and we shared a kiss filled with endless possibilities. I didn't know how we were going to get out of this mess we were in, but I believed that somehow we would find a way—together.

She loves me.

Jack let Abby's admission of love warm him as he carefully disentangled himself from her arms and slipped his pillow into the spot he had vacated. She made a soft sound but settled back down quickly. He rose from bed, pulled a shirt over his head, grabbed his gun and extra ammo, and stuffed his feet into his sneakers. Despite his many years in the civilian world, Jack had never been able to shake his light sleeping habits. He was glad for that quirk tonight. He hadn't even needed an alarm to let him know it was time to switch out watch shifts with Finn.

He peeked in on Mattie before descending the stairs and found Finn standing in the shadows near the front window. A highly decorated sniper with a list of confirmed kills that had made him a legend among a tightly knit group of elite operators, Finn was the type of man who could remain perfectly still and focused for days, if necessary.

"It looks like that loan sharking bastard came through on his promise to speak with the *real* boss of

Houston." His brother's gravelly voice carried through the darkness. "Forty minutes ago, two Russians slipped into the alley. They're out there now smoking cigarettes." Finn paused. "One of them only has three fingers."

"Bet there's an interesting story to that one," Jack murmured as he took a spot near Finn. "How did you know they were part of the Russian outfit?"

"The jewelry," he said softly. "The shoes. The car." With a gesture that Jack nearly missed, Finn pointed to the end of the street. Because the house sat on a cul-de-sac, there was only one way in and one way out, and Besian's men were watching it. "The Albanian crew made a shift change right before the Russians showed up. I recognize two of them from the night Pops got into that scrape outside the bar."

Jack surveyed the situation. "Feels wrong to depend on criminals to keep Abby safe."

"We don't pick the men we go to war with, Jack. Besides, the enemy of my enemy, right?"

"That's what worries me most. Besian won't fuck Abby over, but the other one?"

"Nikolai Kalasnikov is a dangerous man," Finn agreed. "But he's quiet and he's smart. Something tells me he'll find a way to use this to his advantage."

"If there's a power play to be made, he'll take it. I worry Abby might get caught in the crossfire."

"I don't think that's his style. Hell—he came to Kelly and gave him Trevor on a silver platter even when Kelly was training to fight against Sergei. I've seen him with his wife. I've seen the way he protects his friends and hers. He won't put an innocent woman like Abby in harm's way."

"I hope to hell you're right." Jack tapped his brother's arm. "Go get some rest. Morning will be here soon enough."

Finn backed away from the window. "I'm taking Mattie with me in the morning. I've been thinking about offering him a part-time job. This is as good a time as any to make it official. Unless you feel differently?"

"No. I was actually going to bring it up to you." Glad his brother spotted the same potential in Mattie, he said, "The kid loves it at the gym. He's great with people. I think he needs the chance to earn a paycheck separate from his family."

"He told me he wants to move out on his own." Finn kept his voice deliberately low, almost as if he feared Abby overhearing. "I got the feeling Mattie wants to strike out and make a go of it."

"What did you say?" Jack hoped Finn hadn't put him in an awkward position with Abby. Knowing how protective she was of Mattie, she would blow a gasket if she suspected they had been encouraging her brother to move out of her house.

"I told him that was something he needed to discuss with Abby, but he needed a plan before he made his case. I sat him down and explained what my budget looks like and how many hours I have to work to pay for food, rent, clothing, utilities, and all that. He showed me a brochure for an assisted-living style complex not far from here where some of his friends live." Finn hesitated. "If the place checks out, it might be a good first step for him, Jack. Let him get out there in the real world but make sure there's a safety net to catch him if he stumbles."

Jack rubbed the back of his neck. "Abby won't like it, Finn. She loves him so much, and she wants to protect him from the shitty people who would do him wrong."

"You tried to protect me once. Kelly, too," Finn added. "You had to let us go out and be men, Jack. We had to make mistakes and find our way."

"It's different with Mattie."

"Why? Granted, he has some unique challenges ahead of him, but there's no reason he can't at least try. Abby has always fought so damned hard to make sure Mattie got every opportunity he deserved. Is she really going to hold him back now?"

Jack's gut roiled. What Finn said was true, but Abby wouldn't see it that way. Not at first, anyway. Given time to consider it, she would come around but he loathed the idea of being the one to piss her off. "When this bullshit is done, I'll talk to her."

Finn slapped him on the back. "Good luck, bro."

He chortled. "Thanks."

Alone with his thoughts, Jack made the rounds of the house again, obsessively checking the windows and doors. The chilling footage of that contract killer entering that bedroom so easily and completely unnoticed made the fine hairs on the back of his neck stand on edge. He thought about the phone number left behind for Abby and the warning accompanying it. That was a phone call he planned to make very soon.

"You want some coffee, boy?"

The sound of Pop's voice instantly set his teeth on edge. He glanced over his shoulder to find his father silhouetted near the entrance to the living room. "No. I'm good."

"It's going to be a long night. I'll make it anyway."

Jack listened to the old man's slippered feet shuffling away. Though he had turned down the offer of caffeine, he silently accepted the cup handed to him a short time later. Talking to his father was the very last thing in the world he wanted to do tonight, but the old man didn't seem to get the hint. Or maybe Pop did but just didn't give a shit.

"Mattie told me about the watch."

Jack's jaw clenched. "You realize you nearly lost it?"

"I got shot."

"You shouldn't have pawned it in the first place."

"Add it to my list of mistakes."

"I'm not sure there's any room left on that list."

Pop didn't have a reply for that one. He quietly drank his coffee and stared out the window. Eventually, he piped up again. "You sure about this, son?" When Jack didn't answer, the old man clarified his question. "You and Finn might think you can keep a secret, but I'm not deaf yet. I can hear—and I can see."

He gestured to the barely visible cherry of a cigarette peeking out from a tree in his neighbor's yard. For the last twenty minutes or so, Jack had been watching Kostya watching the house. There was something so eerie about the other man. Jack wasn't at all the easily intimidated type, but Kostya had the sort of dead-eyed stare that put the fear of God in a man.

As if reading his mind, Pop said, "That one is probably more dangerous than the hit man after Abby. He's not just a driver and bodyguard. He's a cleaner. He's the man everyone calls when they need to make problems disappear—problems like you and Abby and that camera."

Jack had suspected the Russian could be big trouble. As much time as his father spent swimming against the murky undercurrent that ran through the city, he would know the power players involved. "Tell me about Mando Fernandez."

"He's old school. Well—he was old school. When you thought of a true one-percenter," his dad used the term given to the fiends who ran with outlaw motorcycle crews, "you imagined someone like Mando. He was Romero's best friend. From what I know, Romero did more to protect Mando over the years than he ever did to protect his kid. He left that poor girl to bleed to death, you know. Just ran." He shook his head. "Fucking scum."

Jack's disbelieving gaze slid to his father. Romero Valero was scum for abandoning his daughter? This from the man who had beaten them black and blue while in his drunken rages?

Refusing to have his judgment clouded by anger, Jack asked, "Who would want Mando dead?"

"If it had been a simple killing—a knife or a gunshot—I would say it was a personal thing. Maybe over a woman or a business deal gone bad. But a contract killer? A hit man? No, that's someone who wants to send a message to Romero, and there's only one person trying to get him to listen right now—Lorenzo Guzman."

"Because?"

"Because word on the street is that Romero has been massaging those new family contacts to make some major moves down south. Guns have always been the bread and butter for the Reds. That borscht eating bastard who runs this city opens his pipeline to the Irish on occasion, but most of his inventory comes from the homeland." The old man sipped his coffee. "I hear that Romero struck up a deal with the big boss out of Moscow. He's slowly taking over all the gun trade south of the border. If you want steel, you have to go through him. It's putting a squeeze on the cartel."

"And hitting Mando tells Romero what?"

"That he can get to his best friend in the city his son-in-law controls," the old man said matter-of-factly. "It's a fuck-you to Romero, to Nikolai, and the big boss back in Moscow. So you better be sure you want to get tangled up with this girl, Jackie boy."

Hating that nickname, Jack rolled his shoulders to shrug off the bad memories it brought. "I don't remember asking you for dating advice."

"No," his father allowed softly. "You always were sure of yourself. You were the one I never worried much about because even as a kid you made deliberate, smart choices." The old man's voice took on a wistful tone. "Your mother was the same way." Then with a derisive snort, he said, "Well, except when it came to me. She could have done better."

"Yes." Jack didn't even try to suppress that dig. He had always wondered why the hell his mother had gotten involved with such an abusive, drunken asshole. It wasn't until she had died and he had been helping Finn go through some paperwork that he had realized the anniversary his parents celebrated didn't match the one on their marriage certificate. Simple math had assured him that his mother had only married his father because she had been pregnant—with him.

Jack went rigid when his father touched his arm. He fought the urge to shrug it off or push him away. "Be careful, son."

With that warning rattling round in his head, Jack swallowed another mouthful of coffee and pondered how this might all play out come daylight. He didn't even want to think about the appointment that awaited him at Merkurie Motors. One thing was for damned sure. It was going to be a long fucking day.

9 Chapter Nine

"Abby, hurry! We're going to be late."

"Jeez! Hold your horses, Mattie." I hurriedly tidied up my desk. "We have plenty of time to get to the art center."

"I don't like being late."

"Oh, I know." My brother toyed with the lanyard dangling around his neck, flicking his fingers against the laminated ID card hanging there. I could tell he was trying to get my attention and wanted to talk about his new job. "So—how was your first day at the gym?"

"Busy," he said somewhat dramatically. "We had a new class of bodyguards from the Lone Star Group starting this morning. I had to register nine new guys."

"Nine?"

"It's brisk business."

"Brisk, huh?" I could tell Mattie had been paying very close attention to every word that left Finn's mouth. When the two Connolly brothers had ambushed me that morning about offering Mattie a job, I had been taken aback. Mattie loved spending time at the gym, but it hadn't occurred to me that he might want to work there. I had always assumed that he would take his natural spot next to me at the pawn shop, but it seemed he had other interests.

By the way he jabbered on about his new role at the gym, it was clear he was happy there. I couldn't remember a single time he had shown this much enthusiasm at the shop. A tiny part of me flared with jealousy, but I also acknowledged that Mattie needed to find something that inspired him. So far, the only thing that rivaled his enthusiasm for the gym was his weekly class at the arts center. The same class he wanted to go to, like, right now.

"Abby," he whined. "*Hurry.*"

"Okay." Grabbing my purse, I followed him out of my office and locked the door. Mattie nearly slammed into Jack, who had come around the corner and reached out to steady my brother.

"Whoa! Sorry." Jack moved aside. "Hey, let me talk to your sister for a few seconds. Finn is waiting up front."

Mattie sighed with frustration. "Fine, but make it snappy, Jack."

The former Marine's mouth slanted with amusement. "Yes, sir."

Nodding, Mattie left us alone. Jack stepped closer and cupped my face. He peered down at me, our gazes locking, and my heartbeat kicking up a few notches. "Is it still in the same place?"

He asked about the camcorder without coming right out and saying the word. I nodded. "I couldn't get to it even if I wanted to move it. Don't forget to keep the shop keys on you."

"They're in my pocket." His thumbs brushed my cheeks. "Finn will keep you safe. There's going to be a tail on the truck. There's no reason to worry about anything. You'll go to the class and go home. I'll meet you there."

Grasping his wrists, I held on tight. He had refused to tell me what Besian had asked in return for his help. I hated that I had put him in this position but understood that Jack would do so much more to keep me safe. There were no lines he wouldn't cross to protect me. "Jack, please be careful tonight."

"Don't worry about me, sweetness." He leaned down and pressed our lips together. The gentle kiss heated quickly, his tongue invading my mouth and dancing with mine. My hands slid from his wrists to the sleeves of his shirt. I gripped the thin cloth and rose on tiptoes. His arms slid around my waist, pulling me in tight and reminding me just where I belonged.

When the kiss finally ended, we shared a silly smile. Even with all that cartel hellfire threatening to rain down on us, we couldn't ignore the blissful glow of newly confessed love. Our newfound relationship had been a long time coming, and nothing—not even some contract killer—was going to stop us from finding joy in the love growing between us.

Jack ran his fingertip along the outline of my lips. "Stick with Finn. He'll keep you safe."

"I will."

"I love you, Abby."

"I love you, Jack."

He patted my bottom. "You best get going. Mattie will never let either one of us forget it if he's late for his art class."

Chuckling, I rubbed his chest and stepped away from him. I glanced over my shoulder one last time before leaving Jack in the hallway and heading out to join Finn and Mattie. I made sure Marley, Mark, and our two security guards had the shop under control for the night and left the building. Because Mattie called shotgun, I ended up in the backseat of Finn's truck. Not that I minded, really. I used the short ride to answer a text from Bee and then stared out the window.

Not wanting to alert Mattie that anything was wrong, I didn't glance back at the car that I was certain would be close behind us. So far Besian had upheld his promise to keep the heat off me. My gangster detail seemed to be keeping away the trouble that threatened me.

How long my mobster bodyguards would hang around was anybody's guess. I doubted Besian was going to let this spin out much longer. Having a psycho contract killer running around the city, and the possibility that a cartel and motorcycle club were going to start attacking one another on the streets of Houston, wasn't good for business. Above all else, Besian was a businessman.

When we reached the art center, Finn found a parking place and scanned the area before signaling that it was all right to get out and head inside the building. I spotted a black SUV pulling into a corner spot. The two men sitting inside it were strangers to me, but I could feel their gazes following us until we disappeared into the center. Finn glanced at the vehicle but didn't react. Apparently they were on our team.

Swinging his backpack, Mattie led us into the brightly lit lobby. There were already a dozen or so parents and caregivers seated on the sofas and chairs there, most of them tapping at phones or tablets. Two older moms sat side-by-side and knitted while chatting.

"Hadley!" Mattie excitedly greeted the spunky instructor who was carrying two large boxes through the lobby.

"Mattie!" She returned his greeting despite being unable to see him due to that bulky load.

Always a gentleman, Finn stepped forward and intercepted her. "Here. Let me help."

"Oh. Um—thanks." Hadley smiled at Finn as she brushed some loose, dark waves behind her ears. Those striking gray eyes of hers, the unique color such a contrast to her warm, brown skin, narrowed slightly with recognition. "Are you one of Kelly's brothers?"

He nodded. "I'm Finn. You're one of Bee's friends, right?"

"Yep." She turned to Mattie. "Hey, your friend Ellie is here today. She saved you a spot up front." Hadley's eyebrows bounced suggestively. "She brought you a cupcake from Benny's bakery. It's that cherry limeade flavor. She said it's your favorite."

Mattie's cheeks turned red. "I'm going now."

Curious about my brother's reaction, I waited until he was out of earshot to interrogate Hadley. "Is he sweet on her?"

"I think so. They knew each other before they started coming to my class."

"They were in high school together, but Ellie graduated a year before him. They have run-ins at the rehab center every couple of weeks, but I had no idea he might have a crush on her."

"That's not something a brother is going to tell his sister," Finn remarked matter-of-factly. "It's something he's going to tell his brother."

"Except Mattie doesn't have a brother," I reminded him.

"He's got me. He's got Jack. He's got Kelly. When he's ready, he'll let us know." Shifting the boxes, he asked, "Where do you want these, Hadley?"

"Sorry," she said, with an apologetic smile. "Let's take them into the main studio." She glanced over at him as we walked into the studio. I might have imagined it, but I thought I spotted a spark of interest. "So Bee told me you like to draw?"

"I've always wanted to do comics," he admitted, his voice betraying a slight embarrassment. "I've been working on my own characters and world for the last few years."

"Really? You know I'm a graphic novelist, right?

Finn cast a quick look down at her. "I'm reading your new series, the supernatural one about the post-apocalyptic insurgency."

"And?" she asked as he slid the boxes onto the table she indicated.

"I like it."

She picked up on something in his voice that made her eyes narrow to slits. "But?"

"But it's clear you've never been to war."

She blinked and then laughed. "Boy, Bee wasn't joking about you Connolly brothers. Y'all are some straight shooters."

The tips of his ears flushed. "I didn't mean to sound so rude."

"It's not rude when it's honesty." Her pouty lips quirked with a smile. "I like honesty. We should get together sometime for a drink. You can let me pick your brain. Maybe you could become a beta reader for me."

I realized Hadley didn't know that Finn was a recovering alcoholic. He deftly sidestepped the issue with a counteroffer. "How about coffee? I teach a lot of classes in the evenings so it's easier for me to get away from the gym in the mornings."

"Works for me." She grabbed a piece of pink construction paper and a silver pen and jotted down her info. With the skill of a practiced origami expert, she folded the note into a simple little frog that she dotted with two silver eyes. Giving it a flick, she shot it at Finn who caught it with a smile. "You can call or text me or send me an email."

He held the frog on his palm and seemed a bit taken aback by the woman in front of him. "I will."

Hadley pointed to a big board on the far wall. "We have a group of comic book artists and graphic novelists who get together twice a month. You should come to the next meeting. I think you'd like it."

"I'll think about it."

"Miss Rivera?" A teenaged boy armed with markers waved his hand. "Class started two minutes ago."

"Then I better stop chatting away up here, huh?" She winked at us and started unpacking the items she had brought for the class while telling them about the project they were going to make.

Finn and I headed back to the lobby with a stop at the board where he grabbed a flyer. We found a comfortable spot in a corner. I noticed the way he took a seat that gave him an unobstructed view of the entrance and the parking lot. He placed the silly paper frog on his denim-clad thigh and ran a fingertip along the exquisite folds.

"She's single."

He glanced at me and then fixed his gaze on the entrance. It was a long moment later when he finally spoke. "A girl like that is way out of my league."

"Why?" I stared at him and wondered if he had any idea how high his dating stock was. "You're hot as hell. You're part owner in a successful small business. You're sweet. You're kind. You're—"

"A recovering alcoholic," he interjected a bit roughly. "That's not something a girl like Hadley Rivera is going to consider a perk."

"What does that even mean? A girl like that? Like what?"

Finn shot me a look. "Her name is on this building. The Rivera Center for the Arts?" He shook his head. "Her dad is one of the wealthiest men on the planet with that telecom network he owns. Her mom comes from old school Houston oil money. Girls like *that* don't give guys like me—vets without college educations who are barely holding onto the middle class dream—a second glance."

"That's bullshit." I hissed quietly, mindful of the people sitting nearby. "She's not like that, but I guess you'll never know since you seem bound and determined to smear her with stereotypes and your own hang-ups."

Annoyed with him, I shoved out of my seat and headed to the window that overlooked the parking lot.

My phone started to vibrate in my pocket. I fished it out and answered without even glancing at the screen. "Hello?"

"Abby Kirkwood." The raspy male voice sent a shiver down my spine. "My name is Romero Valero. Can we talk?"

The realization that I had a brutal, machete-wielding ex-con on the other end of the line made my stomach drop like a runaway elevator. "I—"

"You have something I want, and I have something you need."

"And what is that?"

"I'll guarantee your safety."

"How?" Looking around nervously, I stepped away from the window and moved into the corner. Voice soft, I said, "You couldn't keep your friend safe. Why in the world would I believe that you could help me?"

"Things aren't always as simple as what you see on a video, Abby. There is more at play here than you could ever understand. So, if you're smart, you'll tell your Albanian handler to put together a meeting. Give me the camera, and I'll take care of everything else. You and your brother and your boyfriend can go on living your nice, clean life." He didn't give me a chance to answer. "I'll expect an answer by midnight."

A second later, the phone call ended. Stunned by the mostly one-sided discussion, I lowered my phone and tucked it back into the pocket of my jeans. I fought the urge to glance over at Finn. He would be able to read the panic on my face so easily. Instead, I took a few moments to compose myself before returning to my seat and picking up a magazine.

"Work?"

I realized he was asking about the phone call and nodded. "Marley had a question about a watch."

Finn's face was unreadable. Did he believe me? Did he suspect the call was something more? If he did, he didn't push. He left me to read my magazine in peace. Well—I pretended to read the magazine. I scanned the pretty pictures and flipped the pages, but my brain was fixated on that phone call.

Was that the smart move here? Should I use Besian to make a deal with Romero Valero? Should I give him the evidence of the hit and wash my hands of it? There was no doubt in my mind that blood would be spilled if I did. Of course, if I didn't cooperate, it might end up being my blood.

I thought of the note the assassin had left in my house. I couldn't run or hide behind Jack and Besian forever. At some point, I had to make a decision. It just had to be the right one.

When Mattie came out of class, I pretended not to notice the way he chatted with Ellie. The blonde-haired young woman laughed at something he said.

Her response made Mattie's eyes glow with such warmth. It was the same way Jack looked at me.

Though I had always known this day would come, I didn't have the first notion of how to proceed when it came to dating. The rehab center and the support groups we belonged to were so good at offering education and advice on so many topics but relationships? That hadn't been covered by any of them. I wouldn't even know where to begin.

But something told me Jack and Finn would. It occurred to me that Jack was right. I didn't have to do everything by myself. In fact, it was probably better for Mattie if I let other people step in and offer advice and help whenever possible. I trusted the Connolly brothers would do right by Mattie and guide him if he gave dating a try.

"See?" Hadley eyed me conspiratorially as she came to stand close. "Look at the sparks flying between those two. Maybe you and Jack could double date since neither of them have a driver's license."

"God, no," Finn cut in, aghast. "He can't go on a double date with his sister. That's a good way to guarantee he'll never get a second date."

"Is that your way of offering to chauffeur?" Hadley asked.

"Sure." He gestured to the studio area. "Do you need help cleaning up?"

"No." She waved her hand. "They clear up their spaces before they leave. I just need to tidy up a few things, but thanks for asking." She gave my shoulder a poke. "Don't forget that the shooting club meets on Sunday. I didn't see your reply on the emails Marjorie sent."

"I'll check my inbox later," I promised.

"Shooting?" Finn looked confused. "You don't mean guns?"

I shook my head as Hadley laughed. "No, it's a photography club that pairs professional photographers with amateurs. They organize these get-togethers they call shootouts where they give us tips and tricks."

"This weekend it's classic cars and pinups," Hadley added. "You should come out and see it, Finn. It should be a lot fun."

"We'll see."

Mattie wondered into the conversation. "Okay. It's time to go home now."

I smiled at Hadley. "That's our cue. I'll see you Sunday."

"Yeah. Bye, Mattie." She patted my brother's shoulder and grinned at Finn. "It was nice to meet you. I hope you take me up on the coffee date. I'd love to have a different perspective on the books."

"I'll be in touch."

As we left the arts center, I wondered whether the obvious chemistry between the pair would lead anywhere. I hoped Finn was brave enough to take a chance on Hadley. After everything she had survived in her twenty-something years, she would understand the hell he had been through when he lost his leg in that explosion and had to fight like hell to get off the booze.

"Can we have pizza for dinner, Finn?" Mattie whipped his backpack up and down as he walked. Before I could tell him to be careful, Finn reached out and gently pushed Mattie's arm down and gave a shake of his head, silently indicating that Mattie shouldn't do that.

He squeezed my brother's shoulder. "You want to have something delivered or grab something to take home?"

"Delivery," Mattie decided. "I want pineapple."

"I'm sure we can find something on the menus stuck to the refrigerator. There's a place that Pop likes. They do a thin crust that—"

Something snapped and dinged just to the left of us. Before I could even react, Finn had grabbed a handful of my shirt. While shoving Mattie next to his truck, he swung me around in front of him and threw me down next my brother. "Don't move!"

Pop. Pop. Pop.

It was gunfire. Glass exploded and metal screeched as bullets ricocheted off the handful of vehicles still in the parking lot of the arts center.

"Stay behind the engine block." Finn kept his hand on Mattie. "Abby, call 9-1-1. *Now!*"

Finn's order blasted through my terror. I retrieved my phone and slid my arm around Mattie's shoulders, hauling my brother close as I waited for the 9-1-1 dispatcher to answer. Squealing tires and more gunshots echoed in the night. The SUV that had been trailing us slid to a stop in front of Finn's truck, blocking the incoming rounds.

A door opened and a man with three fingers waved at us. "Get in!"

Grasping the back of my shirt and Mattie's arms, Finn dragged us to our feet and pushed us forward. "Move, Abby! Move!" He shoved us into the middle row of seats and shouted at the driver. "Shooter is on the roof."

"*Da.*"

The three-fingered man snarled something that had to have been a Russian curse word. "The girl!"

Finn and I both glanced at the arts center just in time to see Hadley coming out of the building. With the white cord of her earbuds dangling around her neck, she wiggled her hips while locking the door and seemed totally oblivious to the attack happening right in her parking lot.

"Shit." Finn didn't even hesitate. He pushed off the SUV and raced toward her. The gunman must have seen Hadley come out of the building because he fired toward her, the bullet ripping through the glass and sending a shower of shards into the air. Hadley screamed and threw her hands over her head before dropping to her knees. She had made herself a perfect target. Finn was shouting at her but she couldn't hear him.

The three-fingered Russian leaned out his window and began firing in the direction of the rooftop. His weapon wasn't nearly powerful enough or as accurate, but the covering fire was enough to give Finn a chance to reach Hadley. He swept her up in his arms and dived into the building through the shattered window, rolling his body over hers and shielding her from the bullets and glass. He disappeared from my view, taking Hadley to a safer spot inside the building.

I released a noisy breath just as the dispatcher finally answered. "9-1-1, what is your emergency?"

Bullets began to bounce off the hood but before I could say a single word the three-fingered man in the front seat swiped my phone and ended the call. "No."

"But—"

"*Nyet*." He said something to the driver who punched the gas and jerked the wheel so hard I fell out of my seat. I scrambled to get back upright and leaned over to grab the seatbelt for Mattie. He gripped my wrist. "Abby?"

"Just keep your head down," I urged. "We'll be okay."

"Where's Finn?"

I wanted to scream at the two men to go back for him but didn't. They weren't going to listen, and Mattie would only be more upset. "He'll be okay. He's a Marine."

I couldn't believe how stupid I sounded. Some part of me wanted to believe that was all true. I prayed Finn and Hadley were okay. If anyone could keep her safe, it was Finn Connolly.

"Where are we going, Abby?"

I gripped Mattie's hand. "I don't know."

"I want Jack, Abby."

"So do I, Mattie. So do I..."

10 CHAPTER TEN

"Jack Connolly?"

Pushing off his truck, Jack met the questioning gaze of the younger man striding toward him. Built like a quarterback, the guy was easily three inches over six feet and nothing but muscle. He had brutal hands, the knuckles busted from working on cars, and full sleeve tattoos on both arms. No doubt he chose to wear the smudged wife beater because it showed off his ink and made him look mean as fuck.

Jack didn't miss the double-headed black eagle tattooed on the underside of the man's left wrist when he held out his hand. It matched the one Besian proudly displayed. He wasn't just some guy who worked in the mobster's auto shop. This was a made man and a member of the silent inner circle of the Albanian crew.

"Yeah, I'm Jack."

"Ben," the man said, his accent colored only by the slightest hint of Texas drawl instead of the Albanian he had expected. "Arben Beciraj," he clarified. "I'm Besian's nephew."

Jack tried to figure out how that was possible. Ben looked close to Kelly's age, maybe even a few years younger, and Besian was only in his mid-thirties. The numbers didn't add up, but he wasn't about to ask why.

"Do you have a cell phone on you?"

"Yes."

"Give it to me." Ben held out his hand. When Jack only stared at it, he explained, "Bugs and wires, man."

Exhaling in frustration, Jack pulled his phone from his pocket and slapped it onto the other man's hand. "There. You going to frisk me now?"

"You're not my type. I like them small with big tits and tight pussies." Ben angled his head toward the shop. "Come inside. The others are waiting."

As he followed the profane and blunt man, Jack got a better look at the massive tattoo covering the younger man's back. The tips of black wings and the beaks of another double-headed eagle were visible around his thin shirt. With a piece that huge and dark marking his skin, there was no doubt where Ben's loyalties rested.

Inside the auto shop, he counted ten men milling around the brightly lit interior. Most of them were bullshitting in Albanian. Seven of them were wearing Merkurie Motors and Towing uniforms. Even the legit employees seemed to be dipping into the dirty side of the business. Ben motioned toward the group of men, and Jack took a spot on the edge. The others shot him suspicious looks, but he didn't mind in the least. These weren't the types of men he wanted to make friends with or get to know. He was here to do a job, pay off the favor to Besian, and go home to Abby.

Ben whistled and the room went quiet. "We've got twenty-one cars tonight and a special delivery. The GPS units in the cars are all programmed for the drop-off. Paulie and Karl are playing taxi. When we're done, we meet back at Sugar's. Drinks and entertainment are on the house. Okay?" The men nodded. "Good. Let's go."

Jack waited for more instructions. After sharing a few quick words with another man, Ben crooked a finger in his direction. He grudgingly joined the mechanic near a tall toolbox.

"Did you bring gloves?"

Jack silently cursed his oversight. "No."

ROXIE RIVERA

Ben yanked on one of the drawers and fetched a pair of black leather driving gloves. He dropped Jack's confiscated cell phone into the drawer and slammed it shut before slapping the gloves against Jack's chest. "Here. Don't touch anything without these. The cars are detailed after they reach their final destinations, but I don't like to tempt fate."

"Thank you." Jack tugged on the gloves and followed Ben to a car covered with a drop cloth at the very rear of the garage. When the mechanic whipped back the cover, Jack couldn't help but let loose an appreciative whistle at the sight of the midnight blue luxury sedan.

"You ever drive one of these?" Ben asked as he walked around the car.

"Me?" Jack laughed. "This thing costs more than I make in two years."

Ben chuckled. "You and me both, brother." He fished a key fob out of his pocket and tossed it over. "Here. My treat."

Taken aback by the offer, Jack caught the small device and eyed Ben with distrust. "Is it stolen?"

The mechanic and car booster didn't seem the least bit fazed by the question. "Not this one." He gestured to the door. "Let's go, man. We've got to get this one delivered to its owner and the rest of the shipment in the cargo containers across town by ten."

Jack slid behind the wheel and took a moment to enjoy the incredibly luxurious interior. The creamy leather and maple dash accents were unbelievable. He couldn't imagine driving a vehicle like this every day. The damned thing cost more than most Houston starter homes!

He buckled his seatbelt and glanced at Ben. "Where are we going?"

"We're delivering this one to Lalo Contreras. It was a special order"

The mention of the cartel enforcer's name made his stomach lurch. Uncertain whether Ben was fully apprised of his situation, he carefully said, "I probably shouldn't be the one making this delivery."

"It's all been arranged. Besian wanted you on this one." Ben pulled a garage door opener from the pocket of his jeans and pressed the button. "Make a left when you hit the street."

Uneasy and wondering if Besian had set him up, Jack put the car in drive. Out on the street, a silver SUV followed close. He recognized the driver as Karl and figured Ben had given him orders to trail them so he could pick them up and take them to the warehouse after dropping off the car.

Curious about Ben, he asked, "So you do this sort of thing a lot?"

"You writing a book or something?"

"No. Just making small talk."

"Small talk is dangerous for men like you."

"Men like me?"

"Clean guys," Ben said, stretching out his legs. "Nine-to-five, tax paying, middle-class, American dreamers like you."

"Bitter much?"

Ben laughed. "Hardly."

"Look, I don't want to be here anymore than you want me here. I'm going to do this job, and you'll never see me again."

"For your sake, I hope that's true."

His fingers tightened around the steering wheel. "Are you threatening me?"

"Do I look fucking stupid? I saw your brother fight during the tournament. Like I need three Connolly brothers up my ass? No, thanks." Ben traced the gleaming wood on the dash. "I mean that it's best for you to stay out of this life. Men like you have a lot to lose if you get caught up in it."

"And men like you? Don't you have anything to lose?"

"Not anymore." Ben inhaled a long breath and stared out the window. "Considering what Besian is doing to keep your woman safe, this is the very least he could have asked of you. Just keep your head down tonight and get the cars to the shipping containers. When it's done, go home and forget it ever happened."

Jack had a feeling Ben had been asked to do much, much more than simply chopping stolen rides and moving hot cars. He would heed the younger man's advice and give the auto shop a wide berth when this was finished.

"You have the gate code?" Jack asked as they pulled up to the guard station at one of the city's new gated community developments.

"They know to let me through," Ben said, leaning over to chat with the guard. When the gate was opened, Jack rolled through and Ben indicated a smaller mansion just inside the entrance. "That one. Pull into the driveway and wait for one of the garage doors to rise."

Jack did as told and slipped into an empty spot inside the five car garage. Feeling claustrophobic as the garage door slid closed, he climbed out of the car and scanned his surroundings. He suddenly wished he had tucked a pistol into the waistband of his jeans or a backup piece in an ankle holster. He didn't like the exposed, vulnerable sensation that crept along his spine and into his chest.

"Ben! Mano!" Flanked by four men, Lalo Contreras emerged from a side door. Wearing a white track suit and dripping with gold chains and diamonds, he looked every bit the stereotypical mid-level drug dealer and enforcer. "Did you bring back my baby?"

"She's happy to see you." Ben opened the rear passenger door and gestured for the cartel man to get inside. "Let me show you the new traps."

Traps? And then Jack finally understood why this delivery had to be made under the cover of darkness.

Standing to the side, Jack indulged his curiosity and watched Ben demonstrate the artfully hidden hidey holes in the car's interior. The entire time Jack had been driving, he hadn't once noticed anything out of the ordinary about the vehicle. Ben used a series of activation steps—adjusting the temperature, lowering the driver's side window and turning on the radio—to disengage the locks on the traps. One tap of his fingers along the door panel and the trap popped open to reveal a space where money, drugs and guns could be hidden.

"It's nice, man." Lalo smiled as he complimented Ben's work. "You really outdid yourself on this one."

"I'm all about pleasing my customers."

"I'm very pleased." Lalo slid out of his car. He snapped his fingers and one of his crewmembers stepped forward with two envelopes, one much thicker than the other. He slapped them against Ben's palm. "One for the shop, and one for you."

"Thanks."

"You always come through for me. I like a man I can trust."

"Come see me if you need anything else."

"Oh, I will." Lalo's attention flicked to Jack. "Can we talk, man? Alone?"

"Sure." He didn't want to speak one-on-one with the drug dealer, but the possibility that the man might have an offer that would help Abby tempted him to cross that line.

Lalo made sure they were alone in the far corner of the garage before speaking. "Let me throw it out there, Jack. I don't know you, but I know about your girl. She's done some solids for my people, giving loans and making fair buys, so I'm going to be straight with you."

"All right."

"That night manager of hers? His kid owes me twenty-five large on a coke deal he fucked. The interest on that?" His hand slid higher and higher, indicating the rising amount. "It's getting out of hand. I can't let the account slide much longer, me entiendes?"

"Yes." His chest tightened as he considered the myriad ways Lalo might collect on Leonard and Dan.

"I know that pendejo thought he could make back that cash by fencing stolen shit that crackhead Flea was stealing from houses in my territory—houses like the one that belonged to Mando Fernandez. Now they're both jammed up and I've got my boss so far up my ass..." Lalo didn't finish the thought. Shaking his head, he said, "I don't care if you've seen the tape or not. Everyone thinks you have so it doesn't matter, but you know what does matter? That hit didn't have a green light from the home office. It was a rogue deal."

Rogue? "If your boss down in Mexico didn't order the hit—"

"You know Julio Jimenez?"

Jack knew the man's reputation. "He's the cartel kingpin here in Houston."

"He was," Lalo said, an evil grin twisting his mouth. "That tape is the last fucking nail in his coffin—and I intend to be the one who hammers it in place."

Factoring in another power play made Jack's head hurt. He hated math, and there were a shit ton of unknown values in this equation. If Julio Jimenez had attacked without his boss' backing, it exposed the cartel to a war with Romero, a war Lorenzo Guzman probably couldn't win now that Romero was aligned with the Russian crime presence. The drug lord would want to punish Julio swiftly and get rid of that assassin just as quickly.

So who would strike first? Who offered Abby the most protection?

"Give me the tape, and I'll make sure your girl and her brother are safe. El jefe already has men on the streets looking for the ghost and Julio. We'll snatch them up quick."

Knowing that Besian's outfit and the added guns from the Russian crew were the only ones providing coverage for Abby left Jack hesitant to make any big decisions. If he stepped on Nikolai Kalasnikov's toes, it wouldn't end well for any of them. "I have to discuss it with Abby."

"Do it fast, Jack. This deal ends at midnight."

He detected the hint of a threat. "And then?"

Lalo shrugged. "It's out of my hands. I just follow orders from the big boss."

Jack doubted that very much. Running through the intel again and again, he left Lalo's house and slid onto one of the seats in the SUV waiting outside for them. Ben glanced back at him a couple of times, almost as if he wanted to give Jack some advice, but he kept his mouth shut. Jack would have welcomed the younger but streetwise man's thoughts on the matter, but he wasn't about to ask.

Driving chopped and stolen cars turned out to be a surprisingly easy task. After the initial squeeze of panic subsided, Jack approached it like any other unpleasant job. He chose not to think about the poor bastard who had lost his luxury ride to thieves or where the money greasing all these dirty hands would end up and how it might be used. His conscience would never be clean, but he accepted this was the price for the continuing protection Abby and Mattie enjoyed. Now that he knew the full stakes, he believed this was worth the stain on his honor. For the people he loved, he would do anything.

As he carefully steered a sporty coupe up two short ramps into a shipping container, Jack noticed a man standing off to the side. Immaculately dressed in a dark suit, the man lit a cigarette and watched the delivery of stolen cargo. He had seen the man on his two earlier car runs. The guy seemed to be in charge of the show. No doubt he was another of Besian's associates.

"Jack." The gravelly, rough voice called to him as he hopped out of the container.

Getting a bit frustrated with all this talking these criminals wanted to do, Jack nonetheless joined the smoking man in a secluded spot between two containers. A flash of headlights lit up the man's face long enough for Jack to see his black, soulless eyes that seemed so impossibly dark they chilled him to the very bone. They were the eyes of a man who had known unspeakable pain and torment. Judging by the scars on his fingers and face and the wicked tattoo covering his throat, this was a man who had seen a lot of time on the inside of a prison, and not some cushy US pen either.

"Nice job tonight." He took a slow drag on the cigarette. "I don't like allowing outside men into my business, but I made an exception for you. Besian vouched for you, and I trust his judgment. If you ever want to make some extra money, let him know. I can think of half a dozen different jobs that would suit you."

"I'm flattered, but no thanks." Jack tried to be diplomatic in his delivery. His radar pinged this guy as bad fucking news. The last thing he wanted was to get caught up in some perceived slight.

"Can't blame me for trying." The man finished his cigarette and stubbed it out on the container. He pocketed the butt rather than dropping it on the ground. Jack doubted very much it was because the man was an environmentalist. More likely, he didn't want to leave behind any DNA evidence.

"Zec?" Ben addressed his criminal counterpart. "We're all done. You need anything else?"

Zec shook his head. "We're good."

They exchanged a few words in their shared language and then Ben motioned for Jack to follow him. An eerie sensation wobbled in the pit of his stomach as he turned his back on Zec. The man's aura just made Jack's damned skin crawl.

Karl drove them back to the auto shop. Jack and Ben climbed out of the SUV, but everyone else seemed ready to get to that strip club for free dances and drinks. He peeled out of the leather gloves and handed them to Ben. The younger man exchanged them for the cell phone he had earlier confiscated and hidden away in his toolbox.

"Remember what I said, Jack. Stay away from guys like me. Go back to your gym. Keep your woman safe. Put a ring on her finger and make lots of fat little babies with her. Whatever you do, Jack, don't stray to this side of the line. Yeah?"

Jack figured that was sound advice. He shook Ben's hand. "Don't take this the wrong way, but I hope I never see you again."

"Same here, man. Same here."

Safe inside his truck, Jack finally glanced at his cell phone screen. The sight of six missed calls from Finn and Kelly struck fear in his heart. He didn't bother listening to the voicemails. Pulse racing and stomach churning, he started to call Abby, but before he could even dial, Kelly's face popped up on his screen. "Hey!"

"Where the fuck are you? All hell broke loose while you've been gone."

"What do you mean?"

"Someone shot at Mattie, Abby, Finn, and Hadley Rivera."

"What? Are they okay?" Jack's stomach threatened to erupt. He swallowed down the bile trying to escape and hoped like hell that Kelly wasn't about to upend his world with unimaginable news.

"Finn's in the ER getting patched up. It's all glass injuries. Some cuts and scrapes," he clarified. "Hadley is fine, but Jesus Christ. Her dad is out for blood and demanding that the police haul Finn's ass in and hold him overnight."

Gripping the wheel until his knuckles were white, he asked, "What about Abby? Mattie?" Kelly waited too long to answer, and Jack lost it. "Kelly? What happened to Abby and Mattie?"

"They're gone."

Silence stretched as Jack tried to make sense of what Kelly had said. "Gone?"

"Finn said the Russians pulled up in an SUV that shielded them from the gunfire. He ran out to save Hadley and went through a window. He heard squealing tires—and then they were gone."

Jack pushed down the panic threatening to overtake him. He had to think clearly. Taken back to his days in the field, he issued his orders. "Stow Bee and Pop some place safe. Get Finn out of the hospital and meet me at the storage locker."

"Done."

The line went dead, and Jack immediately called Abby. His focus intense, he backed out of the parking spot and headed for the pawn shop. It was time to get that bargaining chip and make his deal.

"Jack!" Abby's anguished voice hit his ear. "Oh, Jack! Finn—"

"He's fine, sugar. He's okay." That was just like her to be so damned worried about everyone else. "Are you okay? Is Mattie okay?"

"We're okay."

Relief washed over him. The vise squeezing his heart loosened. "Where are you?"

"I'm not really sure. It's a safe house. That man from the other night—Kostya—he's with us."

He couldn't have picked a better babysitter for Abby and Mattie than the Russian *cleaner*. "And Besian?"

"He was here, but he left. He's trying to broker a deal. There's a problem, I guess. He didn't tell me much. Wait. Hang on." Murmuring voices carried over the speaker. "Kostya wants to talk to you."

"Put him on."

The rustle of the handoff filled his ear before the Russian's voice registered. "Did you speak with Lalo Contreras tonight?"

"I did."

"So you know what a fucking mess this is."

"I do."

"Listen, get the tape and any copies you might have made. We're scheduling a meet. I'll call with the details when I have them."

"I don't want Mattie or Abby leaving that safe house."

"The brother? Not a problem, but the girl? She has to come. Lorenzo and Romero will want to look her in the eye to make sure she isn't a snitch."

"She's not."

"I know it. You know it. Now they need to know it. Just get the tape, Jack. The sooner this is over, the better. This city is one sunrise away from descending into fucking chaos."

The phone was handed back to Abby. "Jack, please be careful."

"Baby, don't worry about me. I'm fine. Focus on yourself and Mattie." He swallowed hard. "I'll see you soon, sweetness."

"I love you, Jack."

His eyes closed briefly. "I love you, Abby. So much."

He ended the call and stepped on the gas. Kostya's final words raced through his mind. If the Russian was right and the city was teetering on the edge, Jack feared what that would mean for the people he loved.

Eyeing the dashboard clock, he prayed they would make the handover before the dawn of a new day.

11 CHAPTER ELEVEN

When Jack pulled into the parking lot across from the pawn shop a short time later, he instantly recognized something wasn't right. The lights were already dimmed and the CLOSED sign was on the door. During the week, the shop was open until two in the morning. Why had they closed nearly four hours early?

Taking out the extra set of keys he had swiped from Abby's office, he slipped around the back and quietly unlocked the door. When he stepped inside, he tapped at the security system keypad to switch off the alarm—but it had never been set. A wary sensation invaded his chest and settled in his gut. This wasn't right. Marley and Mark were two of Abby's best employees. Neither one would ever have closed the store early *and* left the security system off.

Glad for the darkness that shrouded him, he crept across the storeroom and cautiously entered the office area. The sight of a motionless body filled him with dread. As he drew closer, he recognized the worn skater shoes and ratty hoodie. He crouched down next to Flea and started to feel for a pulse, but the scent of so much blood stopped him. Recoiling, he rose to his feet and examined the massive pool of dark fluid surrounding the lifeless body. No, he was long gone.

Sidestepping the blood, Jack moved toward Abby's office. The bluish white glow of the computer monitors on her desk illuminated the space. Both night guards and Mark had been knocked unconscious and were bound. The safe was wide open with Mark slumped next to it, snoring loudly. Jack rolled the two guards onto their left sides and checked their pulses. Both men were breathing easily, almost as if simply asleep.

When he rose to check on Mark, he spotted the three syringes in the trash can. Someone had dosed the men with drugs. Leonard? If the kid was running drugs on campus for Lalo Contreras, he would have access to them. Hadn't Abby said he was a pharmacy student? He would have just enough knowledge of medications to be dangerous.

Footsteps in the hallway alerted Jack that he wasn't alone. He crossed the room and flattened himself against the wall adjacent to the door. Ready to strike, he held his breath and listened to the approaching steps. When a shadowy figure stepped into the office, Jack launched his attack. Smacking away a pistol, Jack grabbed a wrist and wrenched it back before using his knee to drive the man to the ground.

"Fuck! Jack?"

Besian's voice finally registered. Though he was technically an ally, Jack couldn't pass up the chance to dig his knee in a bit harder. He thought of all the pain Kelly had suffered paying off their father's debt when Besian had them by the balls. The Albanian hissed and tried to escape, but Jack kept his hold firm. "What the hell are you doing here?"

"Abby told me she had hidden the camera. I had a feeling she would stash it away here. With the security system, the safe, and the employees, it's the safest place to keep it when she's busy. Plus the place had already been searched and robbed. The thief wasn't going to come back here. After he hit her house, your house is the next likely target."

Jack eased up and helped the man to his feet. "Looks like you weren't the only one with those same thoughts."

"Clearly," Besian agreed. He pushed the toe of his leather boot against a guard's face. "Are they dead?"

"Sleeping," Jack said. "Drugged."

"Shit." He crossed to the open safe and peered inside. "The jewelry is here. No cash though." Besian glanced back. "The camera?"

"There was a camera in there."

"*A* camera? Not *the* camera?"

Jack shook his head. "I found the same model in the box of broken merchandise in the storeroom. I slapped on a smeared barcode label and put in the safe as a decoy."

"Which the thief took," Besian said.

"I don't think that's all the thief took," Jack replied uneasily. "Marley is missing."

The mobster visibly stiffened. "You're sure?"

Jack wondered at the man's reaction. "Yeah. She was working tonight, and now she's gone."

Besian swore in his mother tongue. "Where are the security tapes?"

"Over here," Jack said, leading him to the adjoining room. He logged into the system using the credentials Abby had let him borrow earlier that morning when he had been reviewing footage from the last few weeks. He clicked through the files and eventually found the tape of the attack that had happened here.

"So there's Dan coming in the front," Jack said, pointing out the older man. The store had been empty inside with one of the guards in the back helping Mark move a mega-sized TV that had been pawned and Marley and another guard up front. Before she could hit the panic button, Dan had pulled a gun and forced them into the office at gunpoint.

"And there's the kid and Flea," Besian said, tapping another square on the monitor. "Looks like they came in the back, shut off the security system, and caught Mark and the guard."

On screen, the two armed men used their weapons to persuade Mark and the guard to walk toward the office. Mark reluctantly used his keys and access codes to open the safe while Marley took the weapons from the guards and tied their arms and legs. She was crying when Leonard made her bind Mark's wrists and ankles. It was Leonard who popped each man in the neck with a syringe, and Flea who rifled through their pockets in search of cash and valuables.

"But who the hell is that?" Jack spotted another man coming in the front door.

"Shit." Besian obviously recognized him. "That's Julio Jimenez. He's the number one cartel man in the city. Well—he was."

"Why risk everything over an unsanctioned hit?" It was the one piece of the puzzle Jack hadn't been able to figure out since Lalo Contreras had filled him on the real situation.

"Family," Besian said softly. His finger moved across the monitor. "Here we go. So—Julio finds these three idiots trying to steal the decoy camera. He pops Flea when he tries to run. The kid drops his gun and surrenders because he's a coward and that leaves dear old dad to try to talk his way out of it."

"And Marley," Jack murmured as the young woman was blindfolded and bound by Leonard and tied to Dan. "Why take her?"

"Because her stepfather rides with the Calaveras club," Besian replied matter-of-factly.

Jack didn't believe it. "You're sure?"

Besian nodded. "I checked it out. Her mother is married to Octavio Ruiz, the vice president of the club."

"Well...shit."

"Yeah. Shit." Besian smacked his back. "We need to go."

"I have to call the police."

"Why?"

"Because there are three unconscious men and a dead man in the shop," he said tersely. "We can't just leave them here."

"We don't have time for this, Jack."

"What if Mark and the two guards were overdosed? If they die—"

"Wipe the fucking camera. Get rid of any video evidence that we were here after the attack. I'll handle the rest."

Jack did what was necessary while Besian made a phone call. He spoke in rapid-fire Albanian, his tone one that brooked no refusal. Pocketing his phone, he said, "Ben is less than five minutes away. He'll take care of everything here. Happy?"

"Not really."

"Where is the real camera, Jack?"

He shoved out of the chair and returned to Abby's office. Hopping up onto her desk, he popped free the ceiling tile above her chair and slid it aside. His hand slapped around until he found and retrieved the box. After replacing the ceiling tile, he gave the box a shake. "Right here."

"Then let's get the hell out of here. We'll take my car."

Jack didn't like the idea of riding shotgun with the mobster, but beggars couldn't be choosers. He slipped into the front seat of the flashy sedan and fastened his seatbelt. Besian punched the gas and drove for a few blocks before asking, "Do you have a piece?"

"Not on me," Jack answered.

"Check the glove box. Take whichever one you like. They're all clean."

He did as instructed and discovered a small cache of weapons. He picked through them until he found one similar to his preferred pistol and then closed the glove box. "You should have Ben put some traps in here."

Besian chuckled. "Did he school you on the underworld?"

"No, he made it perfectly clear that I didn't belong in his operation, and he only tolerated my presence because you asked him."

"Asked?" He snorted. "Ben isn't the sort of man you *ask* to do anything. You have to *tell* him—and maybe he'll do it."

"He said he was your nephew."

"Did he?"

"Is he?"

"In the ways that matter? Yes."

Jack decided to leave that line of questioning alone. Whatever the story, he wasn't getting anything else out of Besian. "So Julio Jimenez...?"

"There's been friction between Julio and Lalo since last summer. Lalo wants to grow, but Julio is easily threatened by the potential power shift. When Lalo put pressure on that prick kid of Dan's, the kid folded and told him all about the camera and other shit Flea had stolen from Mando's house. The rumor had been circling that Julio had been behind that hit and that he had used the ghost to do it. When he found out there was a video out there? Lalo jumped on the chance to take that juicy fucking bone right back to *El Jefe*."

"Lorenzo Guzman?"

"The one and only," Besian confirmed. "Lorenzo doesn't want trouble with Romero. Trouble with Romero means trouble with his partner, Maksim Prokhorov—"

"The big boss out of Russia?" Jack tried to keep all the details straight.

"Yes. If Romero leans on Maksim, Maksim leans on Nikolai, who—"

"Will be forced to get nasty with Lorenzo here in Houston," Jack guessed.

"Yes, and if that happens, Nikolai will start calling in favors."

"You're on that list?"

"Don't you fucking know it," the Albanian groused. "That's the price of doing business."

"But what was the beef between Julio and Mando? What tipped this off?"

"You remember that kid who got run over by the motorcycle and dragged after that concert in April? The hit-and-run where the kid got smacked by three or four cars before someone finally managed to grab him and drag him out of the road?"

"That was Mando on the bike?" Jack cringed at the awful images the description created. "I saw the news piece. He was sixteen?"

"Sixteen and Julio's godson," Besian said. "I heard he was actually the kid's father, but who knows what's true."

Jack couldn't even imagine the pain of losing a child. He thought of how much he loved his brothers and how sick he had been when he had gotten the word about Finn and the IED. To lose a child in such a brutal way? To have your flesh and blood smashed by a bike, dragged down a block, ripped to shreds, and then left to die?

No, Jack wouldn't have hired a hit man. That was a score he would want to settle himself.

"This whole fucking mess could have been avoided." Besian shook his head. "Nikolai told Romero to give Mando to Julio as a peace offering, but he wouldn't fucking listen. No, he sent cash. *Cash!* Can you believe that? Money to honor a blood debt? What a fucking outrage!"

Jack had always heard that Besian and his men were big on the idea of blood debts and their code of honor. "Pop said Romero was always protective of Mando."

"Yes. He did more to shield Mando than he ever did for his own kid. He left Vivian holding the bag—literally—but kept Mando from doing a bid in the pen by offing a witness."

"Why?"

Besian shrugged. "Who knows? Some bonds can't be easily explained."

Thinking of the bond he shared with his brothers, he asked, "Where is this meeting happening?"

"Why? You planning on sending the Connolly Army to do recon?"

"Marines," he corrected. "We were Marines."

"Sorry."

"And yes," Jack replied honestly. "Abby's life is in my hands. If she has to be here tonight, I want my brothers watching her back."

"And yours?"

He nodded. "And mine." Thinking of the hostage who had been taken, he added, "And Marley's."

"You let me worry about her."

Jack's curiosity got the best of him. "Why?"

"Because." That was far from a reason, but Besian obviously wasn't going to give any further details. Jack began to suspect the hardened criminal might have a bit of a soft spot for the auburn-haired beauty. Not that Besian had much of a chance with someone like Marley...

"Tell your brothers to meet us at the lot to the south of the meatpacking plant where we had the tournament." Besian eyed him carefully. "Tell them to stay out of sight—and to keep their weapons holstered. The bosses—me, Nikolai, Romero, and Lorenzo—have all agreed this is safe territory. No one gets hurt to-night."

As he texted Kelly with the info, Jack had a bad feeling that the bosses' well-laid plans to keep everyone safe were about to turn to shit.

12 CHAPTER TWELVE

"You need to breathe."

I glanced at the terrifying Russian sitting in the passenger seat to my left. Kostya spared a concerned glance before shaking his head. "You're going to pass out and become another problem for me to deal with tonight."

The SUV driven by the three-fingered man I had learned was named Arty slowly rolled into an empty lot behind some abandoned warehouses. "I'm trying."

"Try harder," Kostya replied.

"Sorry. I just—I'm not used to shit like this."

"That's a good thing. That's the way it's supposed to be for nice girls like you." He gestured around the SUV. "This world of mine has a way of hurting sweet women."

"You say that like you've seen it happen it a lot."

"Too many times," he murmured and reached for his door handle. "You stay here until I come to get you."

Not waiting or expecting an answer from me, Kostya exited the vehicle. I squeezed my shaking hands between my knees and tried to calm my racing heart. My stomach swirled with anxiety and fear. Glancing out the darkly tinted window, I watched as more vehicles rolled onto the lot. Suavely dressed men in suits poured out of them.

But my gaze zeroed in on the welcome sight of Jack—*my* Jack. In jeans and a T-shirt, he looked so out of place next to Besian and the other men from Houston's criminal element. He held the video camera and scanned the area, looking for something. *For me.*

His gaze landed on the SUV. I jumped when Kostya knocked on the glass. A second later, the door opened and he gestured for me to join him. I slid down and kept close to the Russian's side. Fighting the urge to run to Jack, I walked slowly but fixed my gaze on his handsome face. His encouraging smile strengthened me.

We were so close to getting out of this mess. All we had to do was hand over the video, swear we would *never* speak of what we had seen, and then we could go back to our normal, boring lives.

Or, at least, that was the plan.

"Come here, sugar." Jack drew me tight to his side. His lips pressed to my temple as he wrapped his arm around my shoulder. I inhaled the comforting scent of him, the manly mixture of cedar and denim and leather. "Are you really all right? You're not hurt?"

"I'm fine, Jack. I swear."

He studied my face as if to gauge my sincerity. Physically I was fine, but I was sure Jack could tell that emotionally I was a wreck. He kissed the top of my head and hugged me even tighter. "It's almost over. We'll be home before you know it."

"I hope so, Jack."

"Listen," he said carefully, "something happened at the pawn shop."

I jerked back with fear. "Jack—"

"Flea is dead." He didn't try to ease into the truth. "Mark and your security guards were drugged, but they're fine. Dan and his son stole the decoy camera, and then one of the cartel guys found them there. He shot Flea and kidnapped Dan, Leonard...and Marley."

"What! Marley?"

He nodded and dipped his head, whispering right into my ear. "Did you know her stepdad is bad news?"

My ears perked to the rumbling sound of approaching motorcycles. "Yes, I knew. Something tells me we're about to meet her stepdad in the flesh."

"Yeah." Jack didn't sound happy about that. "Whatever happens, you stick close to me, Abby. If this goes bad, you do exactly what I say. Understand?"

"Yes." I had never been happier to be tucked away in Jack's arms. No matter what happened in the next few minutes, he would keep me safe.

Scary looking guys on motorcycles rolled onto the lot. I recognized Marley's stepfather. He had a long dark braid that ran down his back, so long it touched the bottom rocker on his leather vest. The once-white patch was now yellowed with age and dust, but big bold letters claiming their territory as the entire state of Texas remained clear. He flanked another man—the president of their chapter—and had two others trailing him.

A last SUV pulled up next to the motorcycles. There was no mistaking Romero Valero. Though he looked decidedly more clean cut than the terrifying prison mug shot that had been plastered all over the media in early January, he was still a frightening guy. I couldn't believe that harsh-faced man was Vivian's father. I didn't know her that well, but she was just so delicate and beautiful. It seemed impossible that *that* guy had sired her.

The power brokers of the group walked to the center of the loosely shaped circle we had formed. Kostya, Besian, Romero, and a guy I didn't know but assumed was Lorenzo Guzman stood close and talked. Their voices were loud enough that I could hear most of the discussion.

"Nikolai has extended his protection. He expects there will be no problems here after the evidence of the hit is turned over," Kostya stated. "He doesn't care what happens to Julio or the hit man. He just wants it done *outside* of Houston."

"That won't be a problem," Lorenzo assured. "This has gotten too public for my tastes."

"Lorenzo can do whatever he wants to Julio and the hired gun," Romero said rather graciously, "but I want to talk about reparations."

"Reparations?" Lorenzo turned to the man who had once worked for him and now challenged his authority. "For what?"

"You killed one of my men. The rules on hits inside the city are clear. We need a green light from the council to proceed. After that shit in December—"

"This wasn't my call," Lorenzo insisted. "This was a rogue action that has no ties to me."

"No ties to you?" Romero repeated with disbelief. "He's your right-hand man in Houston."

"And he did this without my approval or consent," Lorenzo replied. "If you're going to try to use this to squeeze me—"

"Hey," Kostya interjected cautiously, "why don't we take this up at the council meeting? Get all the bosses together and discuss it then," he suggested. "I don't have voting powers. I'm only here to represent my boss."

That seemed to quell the dispute for the moment. Rather reluctantly, Besian stepped forward. "Listen, Romero, something happened earlier, and it involves your—"

An engine roared behind us. We all jerked around just in time to see a big white SUV racing toward our ring of vehicles. At the last second, the SUV made a crazy turn and slammed into the line of parked motorcycles. It bounced over them, crunching the expensive bikes and dragging one of them all the way into the middle of the circle. The bosses and Kostya dove for cover, hitting the ground hard and rolling out of the way. Jack lifted me up off the ground and spun around with me in his arms, curling his body around mine and shielding me from whatever hell was about to break loose.

A door opened, and a woman screamed. *Marley.* I didn't even have to look. I knew it was her. Terrified for my friend and employee, I tried to wriggle out of Jack's grasp, but he clamped down hard. Without a word, he reminded me that he was stronger and determined to keep me whole.

Behind us, men shouted angrily in Spanish. I picked out the voices I recognized—Romero and Lorenzo—and deduced the third belonged to an irate, crazed Julio. Every time Lorenzo tried to calm him down, Romero would goad Julio with the ugliest things. Besian interjected himself into the argument, his Spanish nearly perfect, and tried to get Julio to stop waving around his weapon. It was clear that Besian wanted to head off a catastrophe. With all the firearms tucked into pants and hidden under jackets and vests, it would only take the slightest twitch to set off a firefight.

The crack of a gunshot startled me. I jerked in Jack's arms as Marley screamed. Reacting instantly, Jack held me tight to his chest and carried me to a safe position behind the nearest vehicle. Finally able to see what had happened, I spotted Marley standing on shaky legs, her face and hair splattered with blood and Lord only knew what else. Julio had dropped to the ground behind her, his legs jerking as blood gushed from a massive head wound.

Another gunshot and then another snapped in the night. The sniper who had tried to kill us at the arts center was back—and he was gunning for every single person at the rendezvous. Blindfolded and bound, Marley couldn't escape. She flinched when a bullet whizzed by her head, slamming into the SUV next to her and shattering the window.

Out of the corner of my eye, I spotted Besian rushing toward her. He swept her up in his arms and raced toward the vehicle we were using for cover. Another gunshot echoed in the night—and the Albanian mob boss flinched and grimaced. He mustered his strength and all but tossed poor Marley right at Jack, who caught her easily and pushed her down next to me.

Clutching his bleeding chest, Besian fell forward onto the hard ground, his body bouncing as his knees impacted the dirt. Jack didn't even hesitate. Despite the absolute hell the other man had put his family through, my sweet Jack proved what a hero he was by racing out to save Besian. I wanted to scream with sheer terror as bullets snapped around the man I loved, but I just held onto a sobbing Marley and prayed Jack would get back to me in one piece.

Crack. Crack. Crack.

Thwap.

A different sounding gunshot, this one low down and higher pitched, followed a series of quickly fired rounds from the sniper. I heard a loud thunk a few seconds later. Craning my neck and daring to peek over the hood of the car between me and the gunman, I spotted the sniper in question sprawled on the dirt. He had fallen from the rooftop of a warehouse.

I looked back in the other direction and discovered Kelly and Finn next to warehouse behind us. The youngest Connolly brother held a pair of binoculars while Finn rose from his kneeling shooting position with his rifle pointed safely away from us.

For a long moment, no one moved or said a word. Finally Jack shouted, "Someone call an ambulance. *Now!*"

Kostya had a phone clamped between his ear and shoulder when he dropped down beside Jack and started to assess Besian's gushing wound. Beside me, Marley whimpered. I peeled away the blindfold and untied her wrists and ankles. Dazed and in shock, she blinked at me. Her eyes filled with tears, the shiny drops spilling onto her cheeks.

When she glanced at the scene behind us, her expression changed from one of shock to one of utter gratefulness. She pushed to her feet, but I didn't trust her shaky legs to take her very far. Supporting her arm, I helped her walk over to the spot where Besian had fallen. She knelt down next to the mobster and gripped his hand. "Thank you."

Pale and sweating, he managed a weak smile before touching Jack's chest, his fingers leaving a bloody mark. "Get them out of here."

Jack hesitated, and Kostya gently shoved at his arm. "Go. Take the women and your brothers and get the hell out of here. Tell Finn not to worry. I'll dig out that bullet."

Jack gave Besian's shoulder a reassuring squeeze before shoving to his feet. He hauled me up and reached down to grab Marley. Holding Jack and Marley's hands, I let him guide us out of there. Before we got very far, Marley's stepdad moved into our path. Though he was a hard man, he looked crushed by the very thought she might have been harmed. He opened his arms and she flew into them. "Daddy!"

"Shh," he whispered and rubbed her back. "You're okay, but we need to get out of here before the cops swarm the place."

"Your bike—"

"Don't worry about it."

As if these bikers practiced for a scenario like this, a truck and a cargo van screeched onto the lot. Men in leather and denim vests hopped out and recovered the shattered bikes. Marley and her stepdad made a run for the van and piled inside with the other bikers and Romero Valero. The van and truck raced away as quickly as they had appeared.

Two of the cartel henchmen opened the cargo door on the SUV Julio had wrecked. Dan and his son were bound and gagged and looked very scared. Even after everything Dan had done, I couldn't stand the thought of him being hurt. "Jack, we can't leave them here."

He shot me a disbelieving look. "Baby, those two risked your shop and your livelihood. They could have killed your employees tonight and damn near got Marley shot. They made their choices. Now they get to answer for them."

Tugging on my hand, Jack urged me to hurry. His brothers were already in Kelly's idling truck. The moment I was buckled into my seat, Kelly punched the gas and tore away from the scene of the crime like a bat out of hell. Gripping Jack's hand, I suddenly remembered the camcorder. "Jack! The camera!"

"I saw Lorenzo Guzman pick it up," Kelly said, his gaze fixed forward on the windshield. "Not that it matters now. The hit man and Julio are dead. It's done."

"Is it?" I searched Jack's face for the answer. "I don't think Lorenzo or Romero are going to let any of this go."

"It's not our problem anymore." Jack leaned over and kissed me tenderly. "We're done with all that bullshit. It's finished."

Finding comfort in Jack's confident assertion, I hoped like hell he was right.

13 CHAPTER THIRTEEN

After a stop at a storage center to drop off weapons, Kelly drove to the museum district penthouse Bee had recently purchased. The RFID tag on his windshield gave him access to the private parking garage. He pulled into a spot next to Bee's sporty little car and killed the engine. Twisting in his seat, he pointed to the gym bag behind him. "There are some clean shirts in there. You both need to change before we go inside. Mattie will flip out if he sees all that blood."

I glanced down at my shirt and Jack's and spotted the smears of Besian's blood.

"Make it quick," Finn suggested. "We've got company."

Jack and I both looked back and spotted none other than Eric Santos crossing the parking garage. Kelly lifted up in his seat and swore. "We'll head him off but hurry."

While his brothers intercepted the detective, Jack dug around in Kelly's bag for clean shirts. He sniffed one before handing it over. I couldn't help it and laughed. "Really, Jack?"

"You don't know Kelly. When he was a teenager, his socks would get up and walk to the laundry room. They were *that* rank."

I hastily peeled out of my shop polo shirt. After slipping into the too big T-shirt, I waited for Jack. He stuffed our soiled clothes into the gym bag and zipped it up tight. Sliding his hand along my jaw, he held my gaze. "Listen, Eric is going to try to rattle us. He probably suspects something, but he doesn't have the facts or evidence to back up his hunches. I know he's your friend. I know you trust him, but we can't risk it, Abby."

I touched my forehead to his. "I hate lying."

"So do I, but I like breathing more," Jack matter-of-factly countered. "We caught a break. Let's not waste it."

I pressed my lips to his in a short kiss. I wanted so much more, but this wasn't the right time to reconnect. Soon...

Hand in hand, we joined Kelly, Finn, and Eric. The detective gave us a long, hard look. "That's an interesting choice of clothing, Abby."

"We had an accident."

"So I hear," Eric said knowingly. "Is that how we're going to play this one, Abs? All these years we've been friends, and you're going to lie to my face?"

I gulped nervously. "I don't know what you're talking about, Eric."

"No? You don't know about someone shooting up Hadley Rivera's building? You don't know about three of your employees being found tied up and drugged in your office along with a dead crackhead? You don't know about a shootout near the meatpacking plant? You don't know about Besian Beciraj ending up in the trauma center downtown?"

I stared at him. "What do you want me to say, Eric?"

"The truth, Abby."

"I can't."

His jaw hardened. "Jack?"

My man shook his head. "She's right. We can't."

Eric exhaled loudly. "Off the record—what the hell happened tonight?" When none of us spoke, he said,

"How about I tell you a story I heard? It's a story about a video that implicated a certain high-level dealer here in Houston in a hit that took out a biker and a missing stripper. It's a story about a thieving crackhead and a drug-dealing college kid who got in way over their heads. It's a story about a pawn shop owner shielded by friends in some very low places and her boyfriend who was willing to make deals with the same outfit that used his baby brother as a punching bag just to keep her safe." He paused dramatically. "Am I getting close?"

"Eric. Please..."

"Spare me the bullshit sob story, Abby." He backed away slowly and spun on his heel. Without even glancing back at me, he said, "Your security guards and Mark are being kept overnight at Memorial Hermann. If you give a shit, you should call to make sure they're all right."

Feeling lower than mud, I watched Eric leave. Turning to Jack, I said, "We have to check on them."

"You can call them, Abby. The hospital visiting hours are done for the night. You won't be able to get in until morning."

I didn't like it but accepted Jack was right. "Fine, but we have to go first thing in the morning."

"We'll go in the morning," he promised. Taking my hand, he tugged me along to the elevator where Kelly swiped a keycard. We stepped inside the small gleaming box but didn't speak as the elevator climbed to one of the top floors of the building. The doors opened onto a private hallway. There was only one door ahead, and it belonged to Bee.

Kelly unlocked the door and held it open so we could enter her home. The ultra-modern and sleek interior of the penthouse was exactly what I had expected. Bee, Nick Connolly, and Mattie sat on the couches in the living room area and watched a comedy. While Mattie seemed totally relaxed and blissfully oblivious to all that had happened tonight, Bee and Nick were visibly tense and obviously relieved when they spotted us.

Bee leapt off the couch and rushed Kelly, jumping up and wrapping her legs around his waist. He laughed softly but didn't fight her when she covered his face with noisy kisses. Eventually, he took control, cradling the back of her head and kissing her into silent submission. It was the same way Jack often claimed me, his touch so gentle but commanding. Suddenly, I craved some privacy.

But Mattie needed me right now, and my employees deserved as much of my time as they required. My needs and wants would have to wait.

"You missed the pizza, Abby."

"Did I?" I sunk down onto the plush couch next to my brother and gave him a lingering hug. "That's okay. I'm not hungry." Thinking back to the night Jack had calmed him after the brick went through our window, I decided to follow Jack's example. "Mattie, do you want to ask me anything?"

He played with the remote control while watching the television. "Are you okay now?"

"Yes."

"And no one is going to shoot at us anymore?"

"No."

"Eric was here earlier. He asked me questions about the arts center."

"Did you answer them honestly?"

"Yes."

"Then you did everything right." I wanted to ask Mattie what he had told Eric but figured I would find out soon enough. At any rate, I was too tired to delve into the what-ifs. "Where are you sleeping tonight?"

"Bee says I can sleep on the pullout couch if I want."

"I'll bunk in here with you," Finn said, falling down on the other side of Mattie. "But you better keep that snoring to a minimum."

"I don't snore!"

"Yes, you do."

"No!"

"Yeah."

Smiling at them, I leaned over and pecked Mattie's cheek. "I'm going to make some phone calls and head to bed. If you need me, come find me."

"You guys will be in the guest room on the left," Bee called out. "It's the one with the blue door."

I made sure to give Bee a big hug and a thank you for opening her home to us tonight. She squeezed me tight and made sure I knew we were always welcome. Nick reached out when I walked by the couch and grasped my hand. He gave it an encouraging squeeze that took me by surprise.

Ducking into the guest room, I rubbed my face between my hands and inhaled some long, cleansing breaths before digging my phone out of my pocket. An hour and three calls later, I had checked in with my security guys and Mark. They all sounded groggy but were relieved to hear Marley was okay. I didn't know what to tell them about Dan or Leonard and was glad that none of them asked.

As if he had been listening from the hallway, Jack entered the room just as I finished my last call. He slumped against the closed door and blew out an exhausted breath before holding out his hand. "Shower with me?"

Feeling grimy and dirty, I happily accepted his offer. We ducked into the en-suite bathroom and stripped. Jack pulled me into the walk-in shower and enveloped me from behind. Content to be held, I leaned into Jack's embrace and enjoyed the relaxing rush of hot water pouring over our naked bodies.

Eventually, Jack reached for one of the wrapped soaps on the corner shelves. He lathered up the small bar between those strong hands and spread the citrus-scented suds all over my skin. He palmed my breasts with his slick palms and slid them down my belly and along my hips.

Bending down, he nipped at my neck and nibbled my earlobe. The hard length of his cock rubbed against my lower back. Taking the bar of soap from him, I created a foamy lather between my hands, spun around and attacked his sinfully sexy body. I ran my hands over his sculpted chest and down his arms before sweeping them along the ridges of his abdomen. My hand glided lower, my fingers sifting through the nest of curls crowning his cock before they wrapped around the pulsing shaft that I wanted buried deep inside me.

Shuddering under my touch, he groaned. "I need you, Abby."

"Not in here," I said, worried we might get carried away and fall. "It's too slippery."

He grunted but didn't push the issue. Quickly stepping under the spray, he rinsed off his body and made sure to maintain as much skin contact with me as possible. He shut off the water and handed me a towel, shooting me a look that told me not to dally or else he was going to throw me down on the floor and take me right there.

Somehow we made it to the bedroom. Mindful of the others in the penthouse, we tried to be as quiet as possible. Jack guided me down to the mattress, covering my naked body with his and reminding me how powerful he was. Capturing my mouth in a sensual kiss, Jack caressed my breasts and toyed with my nipples. I loved the way he lightly pinched them, tugging just enough on the sensitive peaks to make my pussy throb. His head dipped, and he sucked one of the dark buds between his lips. His tongue swirled around my pebbled flesh before he suckled me again.

My hips bucked off the bed, and my sex brushed against his leg. I widened my thighs and rocked my hips again, rubbing myself against him in a search for stimulation. Jack laughed softly against my breast and walked his fingers down the sloping plane of my belly to the juncture of my thighs. He cupped my mound and stabbed his tongue between my lips, tasting me and making my senses reel.

His fingertips carefully parted my folds. Already, I was soaking wet for him. He tested my entrance before gently sliding a finger deep inside me. A second one soon joined the first, curving just enough to stroke that spot that made my toes curl and my breath quicken. He swirled his thumb over my clitoris, and I moaned his name.

He silenced my low whimper with another kiss, his tongue gliding against mine in the same way his fingers thrust in and out of my pussy. It felt so good to have his digits sliding deep, but I wanted more. I reached down and clasped his shaft, pulling him in closer. "Please, Jack."

"Tell me, sweetness."

"Your cock," I said, practically begging. "Make love to me, Jack."

"You want cum, Abby?"

"Yes." I did. I wanted to feel that blazing heat filling me. "Come inside me, Jack."

He growled and shoved my thighs apart, pushing up onto his knees and moving into position. Cupping the back of my head, he thrust into me, burying the steely length of him in my wet heat. I locked my ankles behind his back, refusing to let him move too far away, and peered into the green eyes that I loved so much.

Knowing my body as well as his own, Jack found an angle that made me shiver. He snapped his hips, driving into me harder and harder. I rose to meet his thrusts, running my hands down his back and holding onto his shoulders as we rocked together and chased the promise of pure ecstasy.

"Jack!" My climax hit me suddenly, the power of it knocking the air out of my lungs. He watched my face as I came, his eyes shining with such love for me. After everything we had survived, it felt so good to enjoy such pleasure. It felt so good to feel *alive.*

Growling my name, Jack slid deep inside me and shuddered. His cheek touched mine as he pumped his seed into me, marking and claiming me as his. Though I wasn't even close to being ready for *that* step yet, I silently acknowledged that when I was ready there was only one man in the whole wide universe I wanted to share that journey with—and he was right here with me now.

Smiling down at me, Jack nuzzled my cheek. "I love you so much, Abby."

I brushed my knuckles along his jaw. "I love you."

Jack carefully rolled onto his back. I snuggled in next to him, grinning at the way he gathered me close and kissed my forehead. His fingertips trailed up and down my arm as we enjoyed the afterglow of our lovemaking. "I know it's been a rough week, Abby, but it's going to get better. We'll get through this."

"I have a feeling it's going to get worse before it gets better," I remarked, thinking of the potential blowback from everything that had happened in the last twenty-four hours. "I'll be lucky if I'm not sued."

"If you are, we'll deal with it. We'll figure it out, Abby."

"We, huh?" I really liked the way that sounded.

"We. Us. You and me." He punctuated each word with a light kiss on my forehead. "Together."

I interlaced our fingers and let the heat of his love warm me. "Together."

14 CHAPTER FOURTEEN

Four Weeks Later

"Hey, batter, batter, batter, batter!"

Kicked back in the bleachers, I smiled as Mattie's voice filtered out of the dugout. He was riding the bench this inning and wasn't about to pass up the chance to razz the opposite team. Eric's players were down four runs in the top of the ninth. Barring a miracle rally, Mattie's team was going to take this win.

"Is this seat taken?"

Surprised by the sound of Besian's voice, I nearly slid off the metal seat. "Oh my goodness! Come here.

Sit down." I winced with sympathy as his jaw tightened when claimed the spot next to me. "Are you still in a lot of pain?"

He shrugged as if wholly unbothered by the obvious discomfort. "It comes and goes." Rather pragmatic, he added, "I'm alive. I'd rather feel pain than be cold and dead in the ground."

"Fair enough," I murmured. "I came to see you in the hospital the day after I brought the plant, but they told me that you'd left against medical advice."

"They were driving me insane. How the hell is a man supposed to rest and recuperate when those nurses are coming in every hour to poke me and squeeze my arm?" He shook his head. "I was better off at home." Smiling mischievously, he added, "That plant you brought me looks fantastic in my office at Wet, by the way."

I wrinkled my nose. "Ew."

He braced his stomach and chuckled. "That's the response I expected from you. Still turning up your nose at my establishment." He clapped when a young woman whacked a ball into the left field and waited until the noise died down to continue chatting with me. "How are things at the shop?"

"They're getting better." Business had nose-dived after all the trouble became public. Though the full truth about the hitman and the cartel hadn't become known, we had still suffered through a period where only our regular customers would visit. "In the last ten days, our loans are finally climbing back up to normal numbers. We'll recover but this won't be a record setting year."

"When people need money, they don't have a lot of choices. It's a nice shop like yours—or a back room like mine," he remarked. "You'll get your customers back. What about your employees?"

I had a feeling he wanted to know about one employee in particular. "The security guards all quit, and I had to scramble to find new guys. Kelly helped me find a new crew through the Lone Star Group. I had a couple of ladies on the day shift quit, but everyone else stayed. Mark is our new night manager."

"Really?"

"He surprised the hell out of me asking for the job. I had expected him to hand in his resignation after he was discharged from the hospital, but he showed up at his next shift like nothing had happened." I didn't tell Besian that I wasn't going to make the same mistake Granddad had made with Dan by cutting him out of a partnership. In the next few weeks, I planned to sit down with Mark and talk to him about his future at the shop. He had been there for years, and I wanted him to know I appreciated him, even if we didn't always see eye-to-eye.

"I heard Lorenzo Guzman made Lalo Contreras cut Dan and his kid loose after a couple of days. They're damned lucky it went that way for them. They were lucky the cartel boys settled for cash and were happy to let the problem slide rather than risk anymore bad press coverage."

"Yeah, the cartel settled for cash Dan and his son stole from me," I grumbled in aggravation. "But I guess it was a small price to pay to keep them alive."

"Do you know what Dan's up to now?"

I shook my head. "He hasn't come around the shop yet." I narrowed my eyes at him. "Why? Do you?"

"I've heard some things."

"Like?"

"Like he's working collections for Hagen's successor."

"No way!"

Besian nodded. "Yes. That's where he's supposedly earning his paycheck."

I didn't want to believe it but acknowledged that Dan had to do something to pay bills. His skill set from many years as a pawn broker probably came in handy in that line of work. "I'm glad he landed on his feet."

The mobster sent a strange look my way. "Are you?"

"Of course."

"Even after everything he did?"

"I don't have room to judge, Besian." My attention turned to Jack and Finn, the brothers standing shoulder-to-shoulder at the dugout and offering pointers to their players. They had risked so much to keep me safe and to protect Mattie. "Dan was just trying to save his son. I can't fault him for that." I paused. "Well—I do hate that he put Marley, Mark, and my guards in such danger. That was so wrong of him. I still don't believe the guards didn't press charges or try to sue me."

"I'm sure they had their reasons."

His tone piqued my curiosity. I noticed the way he wouldn't look at me. "What did you do?"

His mouth settled into an irritated line. "Not what you're thinking."

"And what am I thinking?"

"That I intimidated or threatened them," he guessed rightly. "I prefer a much easier and more persuasive method."

"Money." He didn't try to deny it and nodded. "But—why?"

"Because Jack and Finn saved my life," he answered simply. "I owe them a debt. I know Jack would want me to make sure you're protected, so that's what I did to repay him. You won't have any more trouble over this, Abby. It's done. Finished."

Deciding it would be churlish to object after the way he had helped me, I chose to be gracious instead. "Thank you."

He dismissively waved his hand. "We're good."

Mindful of his healing injury, I gently rubbed his upper back. "I don't care what people say. I think you're a pretty nice guy, Besian."

He chortled. "Don't go spreading that around, huh? It's bad for business."

We watched the rest of the game like two old friends. I wasn't silly enough to think that Besian wasn't as dangerous as he had ever been, but I sensed that our friendship had taken a turn. I was certain we would encounter friction in the future—a mob boss and a small business owner occupying the same area were always going to be at odds—and we would never have the sort of under-the-table arrangement Granddad and Besian's predecessor had enjoyed, but we would always be close.

When the game ended, Besian excused himself before Jack and Finn were off the field. I sensed he wanted to spare everyone an awkward encounter. After waving goodbye, I waited for Mattie to exit the gate. He had played hard and even scored one of the runs that helped his team win. Judging by the big grin on his face and his dirty uniform, he was feeling pretty good about himself.

"That was a great game, Mattie!"

"Finn is taking me out to celebrate the win."

"Oh?" I glanced at the Connolly brother in question. "You guys planning to stay out late?"

"I don't have a curfew tonight," Mattie informed me.

"You don't?" We had recently negotiated a weekend curfew after he had brought up his desire for more freedom. I suspected my brother was trying to prepare me for the possibility of him moving out of our home by negotiating these small changes. While the idea of Mattie living on his own or in a group setting scared me, I also understood that he was an adult who had the right to make his own decisions. Even if it meant I ended up on anti-anxiety meds...

"You won't be at the house anyway, so I'm staying with Finn."

Thrown by this development, I glanced between my brother and Finn. "Um..."

Jack playfully smacked Mattie's arm. "That was supposed to be a secret."

My brother's cheeks flushed. "Whoops."

"What's a secret?" I didn't like being left out.

Jack gave one of my curls a tug. "You'll find out soon enough." His gaze jumped to someone over my shoulder. I looked back in the same direction and spotted Eric watching us. We hadn't spoken since that evening in the garage. While I had expected to be hauled in for questioning, nothing had ever come from it.

Jack lifted his hand, waved at the detective, and smiled. Eric didn't return the wave right away, but when he did, it was with the smallest sliver of a smile that held some promise. It renewed my hope that someday we might all be friends again.

When we left the field, Mattie and Finn headed one way, and Jack helped me into his truck so we could head another. "So—Besian," he said as we idled at a red light. "What did he want?"

"We were just chatting."

"About?"

"Things."

"Uh-huh."

"Do you really want all the details?" Despite Jack having risked his life to save Besian's, I understood that he didn't particularly care for the other man.

"Not really," he replied. "I trust you to tell me if I need to know something."

"I will." Unable to wait a moment longer, I asked, "What's the rest of the secret Mattie revealed?"

He reached out and grasped my hand. "You'll see."

"I hate secrets, Jack."

He lifted my hand and kissed the back of it. "I know."

Deciding two could play the teasing game, I waited until he released my hand and then stroked my fingers up and down his thigh. "You look so hot in that baseball uniform."

He grinned. "I'm listening."

My hand moved toward his inner thigh and up to that thick and growing erection carefully hidden away in his boxer briefs. I gave him a squeeze and elicited a low groan. When I started to unsnap his pants, he stopped me. "You're going to make me wreck."

"Well, we wouldn't want that." I cupped his cock and ran my thumb along the hard ridge of it.

"Not with the three-day weekend I have planned for us," he said huskily.

"You planned a getaway for us?" The idea of sneaking away somewhere with Jack filled me with a delicious thrill.

"We aren't going very far," he said apologetically. "I know how you worry about Mattie, so I booked a suite at the Magnolia. I've already dropped off my suitcase and prepped the room."

"Prepped?"

He grinned wickedly. "We're going to unplug, hide out, enjoy room service, and make love until we're so tired we can't even move."

I gulped as I considered all the naughty ways Jack liked to make me scream with pleasure. I had a feeling

I was going to have a hard time walking straight come Tuesday—and I couldn't wait. There was nothing like being ravished by my big, sexy Jack.

"So what do you say, baby? You, me, and a hotel room?"

I squeezed my thighs together to assuage the throbbing pulse between them and gave Jack's rigid shaft a promising squeeze. "I'm all yours."

His sexy grin did crazy things to me. "For this weekend?"

My heart swelled with love for this wonderful man. "Forever..."

AN Author's Note

Thanks so much for picking up *In Jack's Arms.* If you haven't read the first or final books in the Fighting Connollys trilogy, *In Kelly's Corner* and *In Finn's Heart* are available in ebook and print.

I've received lots of reader mail about Besian and his crew. Everyone wants to know if they're going to get books. The answer? Yes!

The series—called Debt Collection—will include three books: *Collateral, Past Due,* and *Paid in Full.* They will be available in ebook and print beginning early Fall 2014.

ROXIE RIVERA

ABOUT THE AUTHOR

A *New York Times* and *USA Today* bestselling author, I like to write super sexy romances and scorching hot erotica. I live in Texas with a husband who could easily snag a job as an extra on History Channel's new *Viking* series and a sweet but rowdy four-year-old.

I also have another dirty-book writing alter ego, **Lolita Lopez**, who writes deliciously steamy tales for Ellora's Cave, Forever Yours/Grand Central, Mischief/Harper Collins UK, Siren Publishing and Cleis Press.

You can find me online at **www.roxierivera.com**.

Roxie's Backlist

Her Russian Protector Series

Ivan (Her Russian Protector #1)

Dimitri (Her Russian Protector #2)

Yuri (Her Russian Protector #3)

A Very Russian Christmas (Her Russian Protector #3.5)

Nikolai (Her Russian Protector #4)

Sergei (Her Russian Protector #5)

Sergei, Volume 2

Nikolai, Volume 2 (Her Russian Protector #6)—Coming June 2014

Kostya (Her Russian Protector #7)—Coming Summer 2014

Alexei (Her Russian Protector #8)—Coming Fall 2014

Danila (Her Russian Protector #9)—Coming Fall 2014

The Fighting Connollys Series

In Kelly's Corner (Fighting Connollys #1)

In Jack's Arms (Fighting Connollys #2)

In Finn's Heart (Fighting Connollys #3

Seduced By...

Erotica

IN JACK'S ARMS

Made in the USA
Middletown, DE
22 November 2014

15714670R00167